"Are you ready to keep your promise to me?"

"Promise?" He looked at her blankly.

"You can't have forgotten. You promised you'd wait until I grew up and then you'd marry me."

He was appalled, until he saw her laugh. "What are you trying to do, scare me to death?"

She laughed again.

"So you don't expect me to marry you. Anything else I can do that's not so permanent?"

"As a matter of fact, there is. I want you to help me train my horse Star. Everyone knows that you're the best there is with horses."

There was no real reason he couldn't help her out, except that it seemed like a commitment, and he didn't intend to tie himself anywhere, not now.

"I'd like to help. But I don't know how long I'll be here and—"

"I'll take whatever time you can spare. *Denke*, Aaron. I'm wonderful glad."

He started to say that his words hadn't been a yes, but before he could, Sally grabbed his hand and every thought flew right out of his head.

And he knew in that instant that he was in trouble.

A lifetime spent in rural Pennsylvania and her Pennsylvania Dutch heritage led **Marta Perry** to write about the Plain People, who add so much richness to her home state. Marta has seen nearly sixty of her books published, with over six million books in print. She and her husband live in a centuries-old farmhouse in a central-Pennsylvania valley. When she's not writing, she's reading, traveling, baking or enjoying her six beautiful grandchildren.

Visit the Author Profile page at Harlequin.com for more titles.

The Promised Amish Bride

Marta Perry

HARLEQUIN® LOVE INSPIRED®

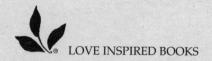

LOVE INSPIRED BOOKS

Recycling programs
for this product may
not exist in your area.

ISBN-13: 978-1-335-53897-0

The Promised Amish Bride

www.Harlequin.com

Printed in U.S.A.

This is my commandment,
That ye love one another, as I have loved you.
—*John* 15:12

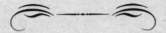

To Brian, my first and only love.

Chapter One

The country road was as familiar as Aaron King's own body, even after all these years away. Here was the spot where his brother, racing a buddy in the family buggy, went into the ditch. There was the bank where they'd picked blackberries, and there the maple tree where he'd stolen a kiss from Becky Esch when they were both fifteen. The maple's leaves were scarlet now that fall was here, but it had just been budding out that spring.

One more bend in the road, and he'd be able to see the family farm. The realization was like a rock in his stomach.

What was he doing? Did he really want to accept the role of the prodigal, returning to the Amish fold in Lost Creek after failing in the Englisch world? That was what they'd think, surely—his two brothers and his uncle. They'd assume he'd messed up, and they'd also assume he'd come back to stay.

They'd be right on the first count—he had to admit it. The memory of the scene that had destroyed his job and the tenuous place he'd made for himself still scalded.

As for coming home to stay...that he wasn't so sure of. To give up modern life, to sink back into the restrictions he'd once left behind, to kneel before the brothers and sisters of the church and confess his wrongs...

The lead weight in his belly grew heavier. He didn't think he could do it. But how many choices did he have left?

He rounded the bend, and the sight ahead of him chased his fruitless thoughts away. A horse reared between the shafts of a buggy, heedless of the efforts of the Amish woman struggling with the lines. Dropping his backpack to the ground, Aaron raced forward. If the horse bolted—

When he reached the animal's head, it was making a determined effort to kick the buggy to pieces, but at least it hadn't run. Sucking in a breath, he lunged, dangerously near the flailing hooves. He caught the leather strap of the headpiece and held on tight, all the while talking in the low, steady voice that could calm the most jittery beast.

"Get away from him before you're hurt. I don't want help." The woman spoke in English, not dialect. She thought him an Englischer, and why not? That's what he was now.

Ignoring her, he focused on the animal, watching the flicker of the ears, the shudders that rippled the skin. He kept his voice low, saying soothing, meaningless words. Slowly, very slowly, the kicks grew half-hearted. They stopped, and the gelding stood, head drooping, shivering a little, but starting to relax.

"There now," he crooned in the still-familiar cadences of Pennsylvania Dutch. "You're all right. Something scared you, yah?"

"Nothing more fierce than a paper cup blowing across the road. Could be he wasn't ready to venture out of the farmyard yet." The light amused voice startled him out of his preoccupation with the animal.

He took a cautious look, his hand still smoothing the gelding's silky neck. The woman set the brake and secured the lines. She jumped down with a quick, agile movement that told him she wasn't much more than a girl.

"Denke. If I'd known it was Aaron King

coming to the rescue I wouldn't have told you to go away, that's certain sure." A hint of laughter threaded through her voice.

He frowned. Who was it that knew him right off the bat, even in his jeans and denim jacket? But looking did him no good. Foolish, since she recognized him, but he hadn't the faintest notion who she was.

"Ach, you don't know me, do you? That's a blow to my self-esteem, all right. Here I thought you'd never forget me." A teasing voice, a lively, animated face and laughing blue eyes confronted him. Her silky blond hair was parted in the center and drawn back under a snowy kapp, but... Then she smiled, showing the dimple in her right cheek, and he knew her.

"It's never Sally Stoltzfus." Aaron had to shake his head, even knowing that after nearly ten years away folks would have changed. "You grew up."

"People do." She patted the gelding. "Though I'm beginning to wonder about Star."

"Your daad never picked out a flighty animal like this for you, did he? He's always been a gut judge of horseflesh. Or is it a husband who did the choosing?"

That gave him a pang, thinking of the little

girl who'd had such a crush on him when he'd been a grown-up seventeen and she barely thirteen.

"Not a chance," Sally said, the amusement still in her expressive face. "Everyone knows I'm an old maid by this time, or so my sister-in-law says. And a schoolteacher besides. And no, Daad didn't pick the animal. Star was a present from my onkel Simon."

"That explains it," he said, with half his mind still wondering how that skinny kid had grown into such a pretty woman. "Simon Stoltzfus never could seem to pick a decent buggy horse. So he passed this failure of his on to you, did he?"

It was pleasant standing here talking to Sally, letting the dialect fill his head and come more easily out of his mouth. And incidentally putting off the moment at which he'd have to face his family.

"Some things don't improve with time," she said. "Like Onkel Simon's judgment of horse-flesh. Too bad you weren't around to save me from myself when I accepted Star."

"You wouldn't have taken my advice. The Sally I remember always went her own way." The teasing came back to him, lightening his mood. "I don't expect that has changed."

"Probably not. Ach, what am I doing?" Her blue eyes turned serious, her smile slipping away. "I'm keeping you standing here talking when you must be eager to get home. And the family longing to greet you, I'm certain sure. I can get this beast home for myself now."

"I'm not in that much of a hurry," he said, and knew it to be true. "It's gut to catch up a little."

"But they'll be looking for you, ain't so? I'd guess Jessie has been baking half the day with you coming home."

Jessie was his brother Caleb's wife, and he'd never even met her. There were two young ones, his niece and nephew, that he hadn't met either. And his brother Daniel was planning a wedding himself next month. Would there even be a place for him with the family so changed?

"Maybe so. If they knew I was coming." He found he didn't want to see her reaction to that.

"You didn't tell them?" Sally's eyes widened. "Aaron King, why ever not? Don't you know anticipation is half the fun? Your onkel Zeb was just saying the other day how much he wanted to see you. Ever since Daniel visited with you in the spring, he's been hoping to hear word you were coming."

He might have known that folks would hear about his meeting up with Daniel at the racing stable where he'd been working. Nothing stayed secret long in the Amish community. Sally was a close neighbor, of course, but most likely the whole church district knew by now. They'd have had time to talk. To judge.

When he didn't respond, Sally grasped his arm and gave it a shake. "Wake up, Aaron. Why didn't you let them know you were coming? You are staying, aren't you?"

He yanked away from her, suddenly irritated. He should have walked right past and let her manage that nervy horse on her own. Leave it to a woman to complicate matters.

"That's between me and my family." It came out as a snarl, but that was about how he felt…like a wounded animal ready to bite a helping hand.

She took a step back, her hand dropping to her side. "It is. And of course you wouldn't want to say anything to me, knowing that I'll spread it all over the community in the blink of an eye, being such a blabbermaul as I am."

The tart tone and sharper sarcasm caught him off guard. This wasn't the little Sally he'd known any longer. This was a grown woman whose clear eyes, showing every change of mood, were now sparkling with anger.

The realization startled him into a muttered apology. "Sorry. I didn't mean…"

The ready laughter came back into her eyes again. "Yah, you did."

Funny, that she could make him feel like smiling on a day when he'd thought he had nothing to smile about. "Were you always this annoying about being right?"

"I guess you'll just have to strain yourself to remember that, won't you?" She began turning the horse into the lane to the Stoltzfus place, across the road from the King farm. "Star will come along all right now that we're moving toward home. And that's where you need to be headed, as well. Go home, Aaron." She hesitated as if wondering whether to say more. "It will be all right." Her voice was soft. "Go home. You'll see."

Sally forced herself not to look back until she was halfway down the lane toward the farmhouse. Then a quick glance over her shoulder assured her that Aaron wasn't looking her way.

Instead, with his backpack slung on one

shoulder, he walked down the lane at the King place, headed for the house and whatever welcome awaited him. Here was the Prodigal Son returning, that was certain sure.

Sally took a deep, calming breath. It had shaken her, seeing Aaron after so many years. Not that she'd forgotten him. A girl never forgot her first crush.

She didn't doubt that Aaron would be welcomed warmly, just as that prodigal had in the story Jesus told. The only reason Onkel Zeb wasn't running down the lane to greet him, like the father in the parable, was that he didn't know Aaron was coming.

Ach, how foolish Aaron was, not to realize they'd be eager to see him. After all, hadn't Daniel traveled all that way out to Indiana just to talk to him once they'd found out where he was?

It was the same with most Amish families who'd had a child jump the fence to the Englisch world. They waited, they prayed and they longed for the time when their child came home. The happy ending they wanted didn't always come, of course. But it looked as if the King family would have their prayers answered, at least for today.

Star nuzzled her as if to ask why they'd

slowed down, and Sally patted him absently. Funny that she hadn't seen Aaron for so many years, and yet she'd known him the instant she saw his way with the horse. Aaron had always had that gift—some said he must have been born with it.

That had been what she'd recognized, rather than his face. Her steps slowed again. He'd looked older, of course. She had to expect that. But she couldn't have anticipated those deep lines in his face—lines of bitterness, she suspected. And the golden-brown eyes that once danced with amusement or flashed with lightning anger were now wary and watchful. The charm that had once had all the girls in a tizzy was gone. Aaron had looked braced as if ready for an attack. What had happened out there in the world to change him so?

Sally gave herself a shake. She couldn't stand here dreaming. She had things to do, and even now she saw Elizabeth, her sister-in-law, peering from the window to see what was keeping her. Suppressing any negative thoughts about her brother's wife and her endless curiosity, she hurried on toward the barn.

When Sally entered the kitchen after tending to the horse, Elizabeth was rolling out pie dough. And lying in wait for her, it seemed, as she instantly swung around, a question on her lips.

"Here you are at last. Who was that Englischer you were talking to out on the road?"

Sally had implied to Aaron that she wouldn't spread any rumors about him, but she could hardly deny it was he. And little though she knew the Aaron who'd returned, she could be sure he wouldn't imagine he could keep his being here secret.

"It wasn't an Englischer at all. It was Aaron King, on his way home."

"Aaron King!" Elizabeth's round face flushed with excitement, probably at being one of the first to have the news. She swung round as Ben, Sally's brother, came in the door. "Did you hear that, Ben? Aaron King has come home. With his tail between his legs, I've no doubt."

As usual, Elizabeth managed to rouse Sally's ire in a matter of minutes. Sally took firm control of her tongue, something she'd had to learn to do since her parents went to her sister's for an extended visit and Elizabeth and Ben moved in. School days weren't so bad, since she was out and occupied, but weekends could be difficult.

"I wouldn't say that, Elizabeth. You know

Daniel had asked him to come, even if just for a visit. They'll all be so happy he decided to, I'm sure."

Ben, with his characteristic slow reaction, mused for a moment and then smiled. "Aaron finally home. That is gut news, ain't so? It seems like just yesterday that we were walking down the road to school together."

"I don't know what call you have to be so happy," Elizabeth said. "He wasn't much of a friend, never getting in touch with you in all these years."

By the time her parents returned from their lengthy visit and Ben and Elizabeth moved back to their own house, Sally figured her tongue would have calluses from biting it.

"He could hardly be in touch with Ben without letting his folks know where he was," she pointed out.

"That's so," Ben said. "Aaron back again, think of that. Too bad tomorrow is an off Sunday for worship, or he'd have been able to see the whole church at once."

Sally smiled. Ben couldn't imagine that someone might not want to be confronted with the rest of the Leit all at once.

"Maybe it's just as well he has a chance to

settle in before greeting the whole community," she suggested.

"Yah, maybe so," Ben admitted. "I heard he was working with horses somewhere out west."

"I don't know about out west, but it looked as if he was giving Sally a hand with that fractious gelding. That animal's too much for her." Elizabeth frowned, then launched on her repeated refrain about Onkel Simon's gift.

"Star was just a little leery of being on the road, that's all," Sally said, no more eager to get on to this subject of conversation than to talk about Aaron. She wasn't about to admit how scared she'd been before Aaron came to the rescue.

"You're making light of it, but I know what I saw." Elizabeth gave the rolling pin a decided thump. "Ben should have refused that animal for you the minute your uncle showed up with it."

The quick retort she'd been congratulating herself for keeping under control slipped loose. "That was not Ben's decision. It was mine, and I'll thank you to remember it."

She was sorry, of course, the instant the words were out, but then it was too late. She sent up a penitent prayer. Would she ever learn to control her unruly tongue?

Elizabeth swung on her husband. "Tell her, Ben. Tell her that horse is too much for her."

Ben, after a cautious glance at his sister's flushed face, shook his head. Then he sent Sally a pleading look that she could hardly refuse.

She took a deep breath and fought for patience. "Don't worry so much, Elizabeth. I won't take any chances with Star." She'd have to give more, if only to restore peace. "If he's not learned to behave himself by the time Daad gets back, we'll let him decide what to do."

Elizabeth still looked a bit miffed, but she nodded. "I only want you to be safe," she said.

To do her credit, that was probably true. Elizabeth had a kind heart to go with that tart tongue.

"That's settled, then." Relief filled Ben's voice. Poor Ben. He only wanted peace, something he couldn't get with two strong women after him.

But nothing was settled as far as Sally was concerned. She had no intention of giving up the liberty granted by having her own buggy horse. And she'd just had a thought that might well solve her problem.

Aaron King. If anyone could do anything with Star, it would be Aaron. Now all she had to do was convince Aaron of that.

Those moments with Sally Stoltzfus had distracted Aaron from his apprehension, but it had flooded back the instant she turned away. If he'd thought the road filled with memories, it was nothing compared to the flood that threatened to overwhelm him as he walked down the lane to the farm. Every fence post, every tree, every blade of grass even, seemed to be shouting his name.

Welcoming him home? Or reminding him that he no longer had a place here? He wasn't sure. Just as he wasn't sure he even wanted to be here. Or to belong again.

He'd have to make up his mind soon. He could only hope no one would force an answer about his plans. Or be too curious about what had caused him to return now. His mind winced away from that thought.

The field to the left of the lane was planted in corn now. Sere and yellow, it wouldn't be long until they cut the stalks. Behind it, the pasture was filled with the dairy herd that supported the farm. The herd was larger than it had been when he'd left, it seemed to him. The barn and the milking shed looked in good shape, tidy and freshly painted. If the place had been neglected while Caleb recovered from the injury he'd suffered a year ago, it didn't show.

The carpentry shop his brother Daniel ran was a new addition. He only knew about it because Daniel, once he'd learned where Aaron was, had written to him faithfully, as had Onkel Zeb. His oldest brother, Caleb, was never much of a letter writer, but that wasn't the reason for his silence. Caleb, with his high standards and even higher expectations of his younger brothers, would be the least accepting of his return, he expected.

Still, Onkel Zeb had said that Caleb and his wife, Jessie, would like to see him, and Onkel Zeb wasn't one to say things he didn't mean.

As if his thought had brought him, Zeb picked that moment to emerge from the back door of the house. He stared for a long moment, probably not sure who it was he saw walking down the lane. Then, with a loud shout, he ran toward Aaron, beard ruffling in the movement, arms spread wide in welcome.

Once again Aaron dropped the backpack.

In the grip of an emotion too fierce to resist, he raced toward his uncle. Zeb's strong, wiry arms went around him, his beard, gray now, brushing Aaron's cheek. The tears in his uncle's eyes made him ashamed—ashamed not of leaving, but of failing to let them know where he was for such a long time. Onkel Zeb, at least, would have worried and wondered.

"Ach, it's sehr gut to see you." Onkel Zeb took a step back, but still held him by the shoulders. "We've been hoping... Why didn't you tell us you were coming? We'd have been ready to give you a fine wilkom."

"This is a fine enough wilkom for me." Aaron blinked rapidly, forcing down emotion. He'd learned, out in the world, not to show his feelings too quickly. It gave the other person an edge, he'd learned. "How are you, Onkel Zeb?"

"Fine, fine. Nothing keeps me down as long as there's work to do. And there's always work on a dairy farm."

"I saw the herd. Looks like Caleb has been doing well." Aaron welcomed the return to a more casual topic. "Still dealing with the same dairy?"

"Yah, that doesn't change. Lots more rules and regulations and paperwork now, but we keep up. But komm, schnell. The others will want to see you." He marched to the bell that hung where it always had next to the back door. Reaching up, he gave it a hearty yank, making it peal across the farm.

They'd all come running when they heard the bell at such an odd time, Aaron knew. He retrieved his backpack, just as glad to hide his face for a moment from Onkel Zeb's keen eyes. His uncle never missed anything, and he'd know the apprehension Aaron felt about coming back.

Zeb had become more of a father than an uncle to the three of them after their mother left. Their own daad seemed to lose heart once Mamm went away, and it was Onkel Zeb who'd stepped in, Onkel Zeb who'd had the raising of them. When Daad passed away they'd grieved him, for sure, but not much had changed. Onkel Zeb was still there.

Aaron straightened. It would have been Onkel Zeb to be hurt the most when he'd run off, he felt sure. Since his uncle seemed more than ready to forgive and move on, he could indulge in the hope that the others might feel the same.

The house door opened almost immediately, and a woman emerged, wiping her hands on a dish towel. "What's wrong? Onkel Zeb, are you—" She stopped abruptly at the sight of him. She stared for a moment, and suddenly her expression blossomed into a smile. "Ach, you must be Aaron. Wilkom home!"

"Denke. And you must be Jessie, Caleb's wife."

And Caleb's wife was shortly to produce a new baby, it seemed. Obvious as it was to the most casual glance, no one would mention the expected newcomer in mixed company until the babe was safe in its cradle. Things were different in the outside world, but now that he was here, it behooved him to keep Amish customs, so he kept his gaze firmly on Jessie's face.

"Your brothers will be so happy to see you." Seizing the bell, she gave it a few more loud clangs. "If only you'd told me, I'd have had something fancier planned than the chicken potpie we're having."

He grinned at the predictable words. Every Amish woman, it seemed, was born wanting to feed people. "You couldn't have anything I'd want more than genuine Amish potpie," he said. "There's nothing like it where I've been living."

The worry left Jessie's face and she smiled,

her hand moving probably unconsciously over her stomach. "That's gut, then. We'll have to feed you up now that we have a chance."

There was a thunder of small feet behind her, and a little boy bolted onto the porch, then stopped short at the sight of a stranger. He was followed a second later by a slightly bigger girl. The boy had to be Timothy, the nephew he hadn't met—straight, silky blond hair, blue eyes that were wide with wondering who he was. The boy was five, from what Onkel Zeb said in his letters. And Becky, at seven looking enough like her brother to be his twin, would be one of Sally's scholars, he guessed.

"Hi, Timothy. Becky." It sounded awkward, and that was how it felt. How did he talk to the niece and nephew he'd never met?

"Mammi?" Timothy clutched Jessie's skirt, and both kinder looked up at her.

"It's all right. This is your onkel Aaron, Daadi's brother. You've heard us speak of him."

The boy nodded, looking at him with those big eyes. "Onkel Aaron," he repeated, but he didn't let go of his mother's skirt. The girl, a bit braver, actually came closer. "Wilkom, Onkel Aaron."

"Wilkom." Another voice repeated the word with a slight edge.

Aaron turned to face his oldest brother, Caleb. He was the one who'd spoken. Close behind Caleb was Daniel, beaming as if it were Christmas. It was Daniel who moved first, throwing an arm across Aaron's shoulders.

"Ach, about time you were getting here. They were all starting to think I'd imagined finding you." He gave Aaron a quick shake. "It's wonderful gut to have you home. Ain't so, Caleb?"

"Yah, for sure." The tiniest of reservations colored Caleb's voice. "Wilkom," he said again. There was a small, awkward pause before he went on. "So, Aaron, tell us. Are you home to stay? Are you ready to be Amish again?"

There it was, the last question he wanted to answer, and the first one anyone asked. *Are you ready to be Amish again?*

He didn't know. He just didn't know.

Chapter Two

For an instant, Aaron felt like heading right back to the road. But before he could frame an answer, Onkel Zeb stepped in.

"Komm, now." He put a hand on Caleb's shoulder. "We asked Aaron to visit, ain't so? If he should be thinking of making that kind of decision—ach, it's not one to make lightly. We will enjoy visiting for now."

There was a hint of sternness in his words, and Caleb looked suitably abashed.

"Onkel Zeb is right, as always." His smile warmed his face. "Wilkom back, little bruder. We're wonderful glad you're here."

"Denke."

Returning the smile, Aaron suspected his brother still wanted to hear an answer to his question, but at least he wouldn't press. Obviously Onkel Zeb still exerted his quiet influence over the family.

Funny, now that he thought about it. Onkel Zeb never scolded or argued, not even when the three of them had been at their most obnoxious. He just had a way of looking at a person and then saying a quiet word. And somehow it always worked.

"You must be hungry," Jessie said quickly as if to do her part to change the subject. "Let me fix you a little something to last you until supper."

Aaron actually found himself relaxing enough to chuckle. "Not just yet, denke, Jessie. I stopped for lunch not long ago, so I'll save myself for your chicken potpie. Maybe I can just have a look around."

"For sure." Daniel grabbed his backpack and tossed it on the porch. "Let's have a look at my workshop. That's new since you've been here, ain't so?"

No one else jumped in with a different suggestion, so he figured he wouldn't hurt anyone's feelings by seeing the shop first. "Sure thing. Show me what kind of businessman you are."

It was Caleb's turn to chuckle. "He's a better carpenter than a businessman, ain't so? He loves the building and hates sending the bills."

Daniel just grinned, his placid temperament not easily upset by teasing. "True. That's why I'm marrying Rebecca. I figure the way she runs her quilt shop so well, she'll turn me into a businessman pretty fast."

"You just want her to keep the books for you," Caleb said. "Get on with you and show off your shop. Maybe Aaron can help with the milking later, if he hasn't forgot how."

There might have been a question in the words. "That's not something easy to forget," Aaron said. "It'll come back to me in a hurry."

Caleb seemed satisfied with that answer. Murmuring something about work to be done in the barn, he moved off and Jessie disappeared into the house, probably thinking about supper. That left Onkel Zeb and the kids to tag along as they headed for the shop.

Before they'd gone a few steps, Aaron felt his hand grabbed by Timothy. He glanced down at the boy, a bit surprised that he'd decided to be friends so quickly. Timothy's blue eyes were wary, but he obviously had something to say.

"We're going to have a new cousin," he whispered.

"You are?" The boy was soon going to

have a little sister or brother, but what was this about a cousin?

Becky took his other hand, not to be outdone by her little brother. "Yah. A boy cousin." She looked as if she'd prefer a girl cousin. "Onkel Daniel and Rebecca are getting married, so her little boy, Lige, will be our cousin."

"That's wonderful gut, ain't so? You'll get a cousin big enough to play with right away."

Becky mused, her small forehead wrinkled. "You mean he won't be a baby, yah? But he's littler than me. He's in first grade now."

"That means you get to be the big cousin. You can help him with lots of things." From what he remembered, little girls liked that.

She nodded gravely. "I can help him with his spelling. Teacher Sally will like it if I do."

"I'm sure she will." He tried to picture Sally as a teacher and failed completely. He couldn't deny that she'd grown up, but it seemed to him she was much too pretty and lighthearted to be a teacher.

"Teacher Sally is nice," Timothy contributed. Then he glanced at his sister. "Race you to the shop." He took off even before he finished, and she chased after him.

Aaron glanced at Daniel. "Nope," he said

after a minute. "I don't see you as a married man."

"That's what we all said until Rebecca came home next door and started her quilt shop. She hired a carpenter and ended up with a future husband." Onkel Zeb chuckled. "Though there were days I thought he'd never make up his mind as ask her."

"I was waiting until the time was right." Daniel pretended to be offended, but it was clear that he was pleased with himself. "You couldn't expect me to ask her until she was settled here at home again."

"I didn't realize Rebecca had been married. Was it someone local?" The man had obviously died. There wasn't another option in the Amish community.

"No. She met him when she went out to Ohio on a visit." Daniel's eyes clouded, as if there were things he didn't want to say. Maybe he regretted not having courted Rebecca before she went away.

But Daniel had been just as cautious when it came to marriage as his brothers had been. They'd lived through the trauma caused by a broken marriage when their mother left. That had been reason enough to take it slowly.

But now that he'd made the decision, Daniel seemed happy. Contented—that was it. He acted like a person who'd found what he wanted.

"So now you're going to be an instant daadi to her little boy. Are you sure you're ready for that?" He said it teasingly, trusting that Daniel still knew him well enough to tell when he was serious or joking.

"Ach, he's already gone a long way in that direction," Onkel Zeb said. "Little Lige was hanging on him in chust a day or two. I'm thinking Lige had a place in his heart that needed filling, and Daniel fit just right."

"I guess it was meant to be, then."

Apparently that was the right thing to say, because Daniel's face lit up. "That's it, for sure. When it's the real thing, you know it's meant to be. I'm thankful to the gut Lord to have a woman like Rebecca and a son like Lige."

Aaron couldn't help but be impressed. It seemed his brother had done a lot of growing up while he was away. "I wish you happiness, all three of you. Now you can use all the things you learned about raising kinder when you practiced on me."

He meant it as a joke, but Daniel gave him a serious look in return. "Seems to me

I didn't do that gut a job with you. If I had, you wouldn't have run off without a word to me about it. I've carried the guilt of that ever since."

For a moment he could only stare at his brother. "That's foolishness," he said, wanting to be rid of the uneasy feeling the words gave him. "You couldn't have known. Anyway, when a boy's thinking of jumping the fence, he's not likely to talk to anyone about it. And it wasn't your responsibility."

He half expected Onkel Zeb to say something—to agree with him, at least, that it hadn't been Daniel's fault that he'd run off. Instead they both just looked at him.

"It was my doing," he said, his voice sharper than he meant it to be. "No one else was responsible."

Daniel shook his head. "It was different for Caleb. He had the farm to run. I was the one who was closer to you in age. I should have known. I should have helped you."

Aaron didn't want this conversation—didn't want to know any of it. But he didn't have a choice. When he'd left, he'd told himself it was his decision. Nothing to do with anyone else. But he'd been wrong. He'd hurt people, and he didn't see that there was anything he could do to make it right.

Sally settled into the privacy of her bedroom with Aaron King still on her mind. She glanced around, thinking as she always did how fortunate she was in so many ways.

When she'd expressed her desire to become a teacher, Daadi had insisted on setting up her bedroom accordingly. She had a desk in front of the window with a comfortable chair and a long bookcase that still wasn't quite big enough for all of her books. The file boxes she used for teaching materials were stacked next to the desk.

Each time she walked into the room, she felt a wave of gratitude toward her father. He hadn't waited until she'd obtained the job as a teacher. He'd shown the family's confidence in her even before that happened. Somehow knowing other people believed she could do it had made her believe it, too.

She settled at her desk, trying to focus on her lesson plans for the coming week, but her thoughts kept straying. The arithmetic lesson for her second graders slipped away as she stared out the window and across the road to the King farm. Aaron would be past the initial reactions to his homecoming by now, and she could only pray they'd been everything they should be.

And maybe she ought also to pray about how he'd respond to them. Aaron had always been hard to predict, like a minnow in the creek slipping this way and that, always out of her grasp. Sally smiled at herself, thinking of Aaron's probable response to being compared to a minnow.

Still, even her brief encounter with him was enough to convince her that the Aaron who'd returned wasn't the Aaron who'd left. He'd had a quick temper back then, but it had been as quickly gone, leaving sunshine behind it. Now—well, now he looked like a man with a chip on his shoulder, daring someone to knock it off.

Maybe he'd found that attitude necessary in the Englisch world, but it would be very out of place here. He'd have to get used to the give-and-take of Amish family life in order to get along. To say nothing of the sheer noise with so many people in the house—two kinder and a new boppli soon to arrive. If he'd been living a solitary bachelor existence among the Englisch, he'd find this very different.

And the King household was more than

usually wound up at the moment, with Daniel's wedding approaching as fast as Jessie and Caleb's baby. Some days she thought it was turning into a race to see which would be first. But they'd cope, however it turned out. Everyone from the church would pitch in to help, and as neighbors, they'd expect to be called on.

Sally gave herself a little shake and firmly removed her attention from the house across the road. The upper grades needed some extra map work—she'd been appalled at how much they'd forgotten over the summer vacation. Still, it was always the way, and—

Sally's pencil dropped to the desk as she swung around. That sound…what was it? A soft cry? She shot from her chair when it came again…a half-choked sob. Elizabeth? Hurrying to the door, Sally rushed into the hall. The door to Ben and Elizabeth's bedroom was closed, but it couldn't muffle the noise of Elizabeth's crying.

Tapping at the door, she called out. "Elizabeth? What's wrong? Are you hurt?"

A moment's silence. "No, I… I'm… It's nothing. It…" The words dissolved in tears. Her heart twisting, Sally turned the knob, murmured a prayer for help and walked in.

Elizabeth sat on the side of the bed, her apron askew, a pillow from the bed held against her lips as if to muffle her sobs. Horrified, Sally rushed to her, sitting so that she could wrap her arms around Elizabeth.

"Komm, now, tell me. Something is wrong. Let me help you," she coaxed, keeping her voice soft even as her thoughts tumbled. Should she run to find Ben? This weeping was unheard of for practical, controlling Elizabeth.

"Please, Elizabeth. Tell me why you're crying. I want to help."

"I'm not…not crying." Elizabeth mopped at her eyes ineffectively. "I never cry. I… I just thought for sure I was expecting at last. But I'm not." Tears overflowed again. "Maybe I never will be."

"Ach, no, don't think that." She patted her sister-in-law, hoping that was the right thing to say. "Surely it will happen for you and Ben."

Elizabeth turned her face away, and Sally realized she didn't want anyone to see her like this. But what could she do? She couldn't just go away and pretend it hadn't happened. If only Mammi were here. Mammi would know what to say. She felt very young and very useless for all that she was supposed to be a grown woman.

"Maybe…maybe it's just not time yet," she said. It sounded stupid to her own ears, but after all, some women did take longer to start a family than others. "Or maybe there's some little thing wrong that the doctor can fix. Did you talk to a doctor?"

Elizabeth shook her head, wiping the last of the tears away with her fingers like a child would. "I asked the midwife. She wants me to see a doctor—she gave me the name of someone. A woman doctor, a specialist. But I don't know. Maybe it's not God's will, doing that. Maybe I should just be waiting and praying."

Sally rubbed her back gently, the way Mammi always did when she was hurting. "Surely it can't be wrong just to talk to the doctor." She took a breath. "Why don't you let me call and make the appointment for you? Then I'll go with you, so you won't be alone."

Elizabeth stiffened, drawing away. "Ach, I couldn't even think of letting you do such a thing. What would your mamm say, and you not even a married woman?"

It seemed Sally had gone a step too far, but at least Elizabeth's tears had stopped.

"Mamm would say I should do what she would if she were here, ain't so? Let me do this for you." *And forgive me for all the times my quick tongue let me snap at you.*

Why hadn't she seen or even suspected that this was tormenting her sister-in-law? Was she really so self-centered she couldn't look past her own wants? If she could help now, maybe it would make up for her failures.

"Please, Elizabeth." She clasped Elizabeth's hand.

Elizabeth got up so quickly the mattress bounced. She pulled her hand free and shook out her wrinkled skirt. "What am I doing, sitting here being silly when there's work to be done? Don't you say a word about it. It was foolishness."

"Elizabeth…"

"Forget it. You must get back to your schoolwork. You can't let those scholars get ahead of you, ain't so?"

"That's certain sure." She knew what was happening. Elizabeth had shown weakness, and it embarrassed her. More than that, she didn't consider Sally capable of helping her.

Well, they were agreed on that. She didn't feel capable either.

Aaron had been relieved to learn that the next day wasn't a church Sunday—he'd be spared the task of seeing the entire Amish community until the following week. If he stayed that long.

But he hadn't gotten off entirely. By noon the neighbors were arriving for a picnic, and there was no getting out of it. After all, these were people who'd known him all his life, and they expected to celebrate his return.

Visit, he kept telling himself. *Visit, not return.*

Wondering if Caleb had any chores for him in the barn, he headed out of the house, only to meet Sally, arriving from across the road with a basket in one hand and a bowl in the other.

"Aaron. Just what I need—an extra pair of hands. Grab the potato salad, will you? It's slipping."

Assuming she meant the bowl, he took it from her. "Can I take the basket, as well?" It was only common courtesy to help her, after all.

"I've got it." She looked up at him, her blue eyes dancing. "I can tell you're thrilled to have all the neighbors coming in to have a look at you."

Apparently there was no hiding anything from this grown-up Sally, so he managed a smile. "I guess I can stand it if they can. Is Ben coming?"

"Yah, he and Elizabeth will be along in a minute. She was putting the finishing touches on her salad."

"Judging by the food Jessie has been producing all morning, I'd say there's going to be plenty to eat." He fell into step with her as they headed into the kitchen.

"Did you ever know an Amish meal where there wasn't? Or have you forgotten what it's like in all these years away? Maybe you lived on frozen dinners and fast food out there."

"Maybe," he admitted. "Unless I've forgotten a lot, it seems to me I used to be the one doing all the teasing, not you."

"You'd best hurry and catch up, then," she said, giving him a pert look over her shoulder as she went through the door ahead of him.

Aaron stopped for a second. If he didn't know any better, he'd say that Sally was flirting with him. Worse, that he felt like flirting right back.

Oh, no. He sure wasn't going there. A few quick strides took him into the kitchen and to the counter, where he deposited the bowl. "I'll help Caleb with the tables," he muttered, and scooted out without meeting Sally's glance again.

Caleb and Onkel Zeb were setting up tables on the grass, and he hurried to grab one end before his uncle could reach it. "I'll get it." He glanced across the field. "Looks like some more company on their way."

"Yah, the Fisher family are eager to see you, that's certain sure." Onkel Zeb grinned. "And Daniel is twice as eager to see Rebecca. He's that excited about getting married you'd think no one had ever done it before."

"So Daniel is becoming a daadi. That's still hard to imagine." Aaron was still having trouble just picturing his brother married, let alone being an instant father.

"Like I said, he's gut with little Lige, Rebecca's boy. The child loves him already, and Rebecca... Well, you'll see the way they look at each other." Onkel Zeb gave him a sly glance. "Seems to me it's become a tradition, the King boys getting married."

"Count me out," he said quickly. "It's not for me." Sally's lively face appeared in his mind's eye, and he chased it away.

"More work, less talk," Caleb said. "There's still the benches to set up."

"Right." Aaron picked up one of the benches

and carried it to its proper place. He'd be just as happy to have enough jobs to keep him from needless conversation with the neighbors, but he didn't guess that was possible.

In any event, meeting and greeting wasn't as difficult as Aaron had expected, even though he felt foolishly awkward at times. Mostly people hadn't changed much—just gotten older. There was Sam Fisher from next door, who was Caleb's age and had a flock of kids already. He and his Leah must have married early, since their oldest boy was a gangly youth entering his teens and looking much as Sam had at that age.

Daniel's Rebecca had grown up into a beauty, that was for sure. Not lively, like Sally, but with a serene calm that turned into joy each time her eyes met Daniel's. It was oddly disturbing to see that flare of love returned by his easygoing brother. Lige, the little boy, seemed attached to Daniel's pant leg most of the time, chattering away a mile a minute.

Onkel Zeb caught him watching Daniel and Rebecca. "They're gut together, yah? It's a wonder to see Daniel so happy, and Rebecca, too."

"I'm still trying to get used to Caleb being married and having a family. Now Daniel."

He shook his head. "I'm not sure what kind of an uncle I'm going to be, but I'm certain sure I won't do as gut a job as you did with us."

"It'll come to you," his uncle said. "Most things are natural when it's family."

He wasn't so convinced of that, but he could hardly argue with his uncle after all Zeb had done for them. His gaze strayed to Sally's brother, Ben, and his wife.

"Ben hasn't changed," he said. "His wife…"

Onkel Zeb grinned. "Tried to get your whole life story out of you, did she? Ach, Elizabeth's a gut woman, but she has an opinion on everything. I expect she and Sally are butting heads plenty these days. Elizabeth and Ben are staying in the farmhouse with Sally while her and Ben's folks are away."

"Sally said something about it." And based on his brief encounter with Elizabeth, he could understand if she got on Sally's nerves.

"Speaking of Sally, here she is," Zeb said. "Are you looking for me or for my handsome nephew, Teacher Sally?"

Sally smiled, squeezing his arm. "You're my sweetheart, Zeb. But it's Aaron I need to see at the moment."

Still trying to get used to the grown-up Sally, he couldn't find a response for a second or two—long enough for Onkel Zeb to move off. "I'll leave you to talk about it, then."

"I'm not sure what…" he began, but Sally plunged right in.

"Komm, now, Aaron. I thought you might be ready to keep your promise to me."

"Promise?" He looked at her blankly.

"You can't have forgotten. You promised you'd wait until I grew up and then you'd marry me."

He stared at her, appalled for what seemed forever until he saw the laughter in her eyes. "Sally Stoltzfus, you've turned into a threat to my sanity. What are you trying to do, scare me to death?"

She gave a gurgle of laughter. "You looked a little bored with the picnic. I thought I'd wake you up."

"Not bored," he said quickly. "Just…trying to find my way. So you don't expect me to marry you. Anything else I can do that's not so permanent?"

"As a matter of fact, there is. I want you to help me train Star."

So that was it. He frowned, trying to think of a way to refuse that wouldn't hurt her feelings.

"You saw what Star is like," she went on

without waiting for an answer. "I've got to get him trained, and soon. And everyone knows that you're the best there is with horses."

"I don't think everyone believes any such thing," he retorted. "They don't know me well enough anymore."

She waved that away. "You've been working with horses while you were gone. And Zeb always says you were born with the gift."

"Onkel Zeb might be a little bit prejudiced," he said, trying to organize his thoughts. There was no real reason he couldn't help her out, except that it seemed like a commitment, and he didn't intend to tie himself anywhere, not now.

"You can't deny that Star needs help, can you?" Her laughing gaze invited him to share her memory of the previous day.

"He needs help all right, but I don't quite see the point. Can't you use the family buggy when you need it?" He suspected that if he didn't come up with a good reason, he'd find himself working with that flighty gelding.

Her face grew serious suddenly. "As long as I do that, I'm depending on someone else. I want to make my own decisions about when and where I'm going. I'd like to be a bit independent, at least in that. I thought you were the one person who might understand."

That hit him right where he lived. He did understand—that was the trouble. He understood too well, and it made him vulnerable where Sally was concerned. He fumbled for words. "I'd like to help. But I don't know how long I'll be here and—"

"That doesn't matter." Seeing her face change was like watching the sun come out. "I'll take whatever time you can spare. Denke, Aaron. I'm wonderful glad."

He started to say that his words hadn't been a yes, but before he could, Sally had grabbed his hand and every thought flew right out of his head.

It was just like her catching hold of Onkel Zeb's arm, he tried to tell himself. But it didn't work. When she touched him, something seemed to light between them like a spark arcing from one terminal to another. He felt it right down to his toes, and he knew in that instant that he was in trouble.

Chapter Three

Sally found herself fumbling for words. Her brain seemed to have stopped working the instant her hand touched Aaron. That sudden flare of something between them…had he felt it, too? Or was she imagining it? Finally she managed to mutter something.

"Denke, Aaron." Then she fled.

By the time she'd reached the tables, she'd grabbed hold of her self-control. All she could think was that it was good she'd gotten Aaron's agreement before she'd become too tongue-tied to say a word, let alone convince anyone of anything.

Imagine Sally Stoltzfus speechless—no one who knew her would believe it.

She kept walking, moving around the tables and picking up used dishes, mainly because she didn't want to talk to anyone just now. What she needed was a scolding for her foolishness, but only from herself. No one else must know about that abrupt, startling stroke of attraction she'd felt when she'd touched Aaron.

And what were you doing touching him? She'd hadn't thought—she'd just acted out of impulsive gratitude that he seemed willing to help her. And now this happened.

It had been a long time since she'd experienced that wave of…what? Infatuation? She supposed that was it. After what had happened with Frederick Yoder, she'd armored herself against such a thing. After all, for a decent Amish girl to get right up to a few weeks before her wedding and then back out didn't do her reputation any good. She certainly couldn't let any more rumors start about her.

But what else could she have done about Frederick? She'd let herself be carried along on a wave of feeling, happy because everyone else seemed happy for her. Then quite suddenly, between one moment and the next, she'd known it was no good. She liked Fred. He was a fine person. But when she'd thought seriously about spending the rest of her life with him she'd known it wasn't enough.

Mamm and Daad hadn't understood, she suspected, but they'd never let that show. They'd stood by her, apologized to everyone involved and quietly set about the task of living it down.

It had taken some doing, she knew. There were probably still those who blamed her for what she'd done, despite the fact that Fred was happily married now and the father of twins. But the experience had left her wary, and now she had to go and let her guard down. And with Aaron King, of all people.

What if he'd known? Struck with the thought, she stood stock-still, holding an armful of dishes. If she had given herself away, if Aaron had realized what she'd felt—

"Sally, you're looking very red in the face. What's wrong?"

It was Elizabeth, and she couldn't let her guess the reason for her embarrassment.

"It's a hot day for October, ain't so? I was in the sun too long, I think. I'll just take these things into the kitchen."

She hurried toward the house, praying no one would follow her. And that no one was watching her and wondering.

Foolish, so foolish. If Aaron had recognized her reaction to simply touching his hand, there was no doubt what he'd think. He'd be smiling, telling himself she was still the silly little girl who'd had a crush on him all those years ago. Worse, she was starting to feel like that girl, her hard-won poise escaping her.

When the kitchen door closed behind her, Sally let out a sigh of relief. Jessie, sitting at the table, started to get up.

A glance at Jessie's pallor was enough to tell Sally that Jessie had been overdoing it. She put the dishes on the counter and hurried to push her gently back into her chair. First Elizabeth, and now Jessie, driving her into situations she didn't feel ready for.

"Ach, it's that hot out today for October, ain't so?" She talked to cover her concern. "Tires you out, I know. You just sit still, and I'll get you a cool drink. Unless you want Caleb…"

"No, no, don't tell Caleb." Jessie sank back into her seat. "I don't want anyone upset just because I'm a little tired. You won't say anything, will you, Sally?"

"Not if you don't want me to." She was already pouring a glass of cold lemonade. "It seems to me you deserve some fussing over just now, but if you don't want it, that's fine with me." She set the lemonade glass on the table in front of Jessie. "I can understand not wanting all the women clucking over you."

"That's it." Jessie sipped the lemonade. "Goodness, I'm never sick. And I certain sure don't want to make a fuss over something as natural as having a baby. But I confess, I do seem to need a little more rest than usual."

"Well, you just sit there and relax. No need to talk, even." Sally turned the water on and added detergent to the sink. "Pretend I'm not here."

"Denke, Sally. Maybe I will." She leaned back in the chair.

If she were the one expecting a baby, Sally rather thought she'd welcome a little extra fussing over. But Jessie was so determinedly practical and sensible. Sometimes Sally wondered if she was trying hard to be different from the flighty woman, now deceased, who'd been Caleb's first wife.

She swished suds over a serving platter. If she were a bit wiser, maybe she could come up with something comforting to say. Once again, as with Elizabeth, she didn't have the right words.

From the window over the sink, she had a good view of part of the backyard. It just so happened that it was the part that included

Aaron. Well, at least here she could watch him without anyone noticing.

If he'd been at all ruffled by what had happened between them, it didn't show. He was smiling at something his little niece had said, his face relaxing. So at least he could relax, when he tried. She'd begun to wonder if that forbidding expression was permanent. Something unpleasant must have put those lines in his face.

Aaron had always been appealing to the girls, maybe especially because they never knew where they were with him. Now he'd added a dangerous edge that ought to warn away any sensible woman. But women were seldom sensible about things like that.

"How is it going since Aaron got here?" she asked, impulse getting the better of her. "I'm sure it was a shock, even if a happy one."

"Yah, that's so." Jessie moved her glass in slow circles on the tabletop, scarred with generations of use. She seemed intent on the pattern of moisture she made. "It's wonderful gut he came home. Everybody feels that way." She almost sounded as if she were arguing with herself.

Sally thought she knew why. Whatever else he might be, Aaron had never exactly been a peacemaker. He'd always been quick to flare up. His sojourn in the Englisch world might have taught him to control that, but somehow she didn't think anyone could count on it.

"Still, it makes a difference, having an extra person in the house. Adds to your work, I'm sure."

"That's no matter," Jessie said quickly, looking up. "I don't grudge an instant of it, and besides, Onkel Zeb is so much help to me." Her face crinkled. "As much help as having another woman in the house, though he wouldn't want to hear me say so."

Sally grinned. "He might not mind. He was pretty much mother and father to those boys after their mamm left."

"That's so." She hesitated, but there was something in her expression that seemed wary. "I worry too much, I know."

All at once Sally knew what it was that put that look in Jessie's eyes. She was worried about Caleb. She must know that it had apparently been Aaron's frequent clashes with Caleb that had led to his going away the first time.

And if the same thing happened again, would Aaron respond in the same way? Would he go away again, for good this time?

* * *

The picnic finally started to wind down, much to Aaron's relief. He was growing tired of answering the same questions over and over. Or maybe tired of evading the answers. Obviously folks who had known him all his life thought they were entitled to hear about his time in the outside world, even if he wasn't ready to talk about it.

If…and it was a big if…he decided he wanted to stay, to become Amish again… well, that would mean kneeling in front of the whole church to confess his wrongs and ask forgiveness. The very thought made his stomach queasy.

He couldn't. It was impossible. The Englisch world wouldn't expect such a thing, but being Amish was to be different. To live by Scripture and the rules of the community. *Impossible*, he told himself again.

Aaron yanked himself out of his self-absorption and hurried to help Onkel Zeb. He and the two children were starting to take the tables down, and he reached them just in time to give his small nephew a helping hand.

The boy frowned. "I have it."

"Sure you do," he said easily. "But I'd best

help, or Onkel Zeb might scold me for not doing my part."

Timothy giggled. "He wouldn't scold you."

"Sure I would. He's part of the family, ain't so? When he was a boy like you, I had to scold him plenty." Onkel Zeb hefted the table with surprising ease. He might have aged in appearance, but the strength of his lean, wiry body hadn't changed.

The boy's eyes grew wide. "Was he very naughty?"

"Yah, I was," Aaron said. The child didn't know the half of it. "Sometimes I'd think no one had noticed something I did, but Onkel Zeb always knew. Eyes in the back of his head, I guess."

Timothy gave Onkel Zeb an awed look, and Zeb laughed, shaking his head. "It's just an expression, Timothy. I don't need an extra pair of eyes but I know young ones."

Becky nodded, as if she'd had experiences of her own with Onkel Zeb. She shook the tablecloth out. "Shall I take this in to Mammi?"

At his nod, Becky ran toward the house, taking it for granted that she would help. Caleb's young ones were being raised with a sense of responsibility, it seemed.

"Many hands make light work, yah?" Onkel Zeb said, as if he'd known what Aaron was thinking.

"Are we going to take the tables to the shed?" Timothy flexed his muscles. "I can help."

"We'll just stack them here and put them away later, I think," Onkel Zeb said tactfully. "How about you help your sister clean off the other table? Then we'll soon be done."

Nodding, Timothy scampered off, and Aaron found himself smiling. "They're gut kids. And Caleb is fortunate."

"Yah, that's so. Seems funny when you think that folks used to say that the King men weren't destined for true love. Now Caleb is happily married and Daniel soon to follow."

He'd forgotten that people had once talked that way. Well, his brothers had proved them wrong.

Onkel Zeb raised his eyebrows at Aaron. "And what about you? Is there no woman in your life?"

Aaron shrugged. "Not now." He evaded his uncle's gaze.

"But there was?" Zeb was gently persistent.

"There was." Aaron swung a bench onto the stack of tables. "Not anymore."

The words were enough to put a bad taste

in his mouth. He'd thought Diana Lang cared about him. Turned out all she'd cared about was luring him away to train horses for her employer. It was actually kind of flattering, he supposed, that George Norton wanted his services as a trainer enough to go that far. But sulky racing was as competitive as any kind of racing, he guessed.

Maybe he hadn't actually been in love with Diana, but betrayal hurt anyway. To say nothing of humiliation.

Onkel Zeb had said nothing more, but he'd been studying Aaron's face. And Aaron suspected he was coming to his own conclusions. He always did, as much by what Aaron didn't say as by what he did say.

"Maybe you weren't meant to marry an Englischer," Onkel Zeb said at last. "Now that you're home, you'd maybe find someone a lot more suitable as a wife."

Was he thinking of Sally? Granted that his uncle had a gift for knowing what was going on in his nephews' minds, he surely couldn't think that. How could he know about that brief moment of attraction between him and Sally? No, he couldn't.

"I'm a long way from that. I'm not thinking any farther than a visit right now. Just...

don't count on my staying. I don't know that it'll happen."

Onkel Zeb didn't seem perturbed. "Listen for God's voice. He'll make it clear, if you'll only listen."

The children came running back at that point, so Aaron didn't have to come up with an answer. Good thing, since he didn't have one.

"We're all finished," Becky announced.

"Gut job. Work is easy because everyone in the family does his or her share, ain't so?"

Aaron didn't know if that was aimed at him or not, but he figured he ought to make an effort. "Think I'll go see if Caleb will let me help with the milking. I believe I remember enough to be useful."

"Yah, you don't forget the things you learned as a boy." His uncle seemed pleased.

"I'll go with you, Onkel Aaron." Timothy grabbed his hand. "Sometimes I get to help a little. Daadi says when I'm bigger I can take over. How big do you think I'll have to be?"

"However big your daadi says," he replied. He wasn't going to start an argument by offering an opinion if he could help it.

Timothy didn't seem upset at the nonanswer. Maybe he hadn't expected anything else.

He skipped alongside Aaron, chattering about the dairy herd and how he might have a calf to raise all by himself in the spring.

A nice kid. Caleb had done a fine job with his two, despite the problems caused by his first wife. They seemed to consider Jessie their mammi now, and maybe they didn't even remember much else. From what he'd seen so far, they couldn't ask for someone better. Jessie loved them and took care of them as if they were her own.

How different might his life have been if their father had remarried after they'd learned that their mother had died? But it probably was too late then. He'd already withdrawn from life when she left.

It was impossible to guess how different things might have been. Anyway, they'd had Onkel Zeb, and they'd gotten along all right, hadn't they?

Caleb might have suffered the most, he saw now that he looked at it from an adult viewpoint. He'd not only lost his mother and found his father unreachable, but he'd taken over responsibility for the dairy farm long before he'd normally have been expected to.

Aaron had never thought of feeling sorry for the big brother who'd bossed him around and always seemed so sure of himself. Funny that coming back was changing his ideas about a lot of things.

"Timothy? What are you doing?" Caleb's voice had an edge to it when he turned around and saw them together, and the sympathy Aaron had been feeling vanished.

Timothy didn't seem to notice, because he trotted to his father. "I brought Onkel Aaron to help with the milking, Daadi. He says he remembers how to do it."

"He does, does he?" Caleb patted his head. "We'll have to see if he really does, ain't so?"

Timothy grinned, maybe seeing it as a joke. But Aaron didn't like the measuring way Caleb was looking at him. More, he didn't think it had anything to do with whether or not he could help with the milking.

Caleb hadn't liked seeing his son chattering away to his renegade brother. Well, if that was how he felt about it, then it didn't matter how many times Caleb said he was welcome here, because Aaron would know it wasn't true. Bitterness took another bite out of his heart.

Sally walked home from school on Monday afternoon, with Becky and young Lige Mast skipping alongside her. Lige's older cousins were ahead of them, girls with their heads together, sharing secrets. The boys kicked stones as they went along, playing some game of their own.

Some things never changed. Sally smiled. This little parade of scholars might just as easily have been her, her brothers and sisters, the King boys, and the other neighboring kids, all walking along this same road years ago. As they came to each lane, a few would peel off for home. She glanced at the youngest two walking beside her.

"Don't forget to show your mammi the star you got on your spelling paper, Becky. And Lige, your mammi will be so pleased with the autumn picture you made." Lige had adjusted well to his new life, but he was still a little shy, and she tried always to give him a little extra reassurance.

"I'll show her first thing, Teacher Sally." Becky was looking pleased with herself. "Timothy says he wants to start school so he can get stars on his papers, too."

"I'm sure he will." She hoped so, anyway. Becky was a natural scholar with a love for reading that helped with her schoolwork. Sally would have to find out what young Timothy did well, so she could encourage him.

Lige didn't speak, but he smiled as he looked at the picture he held in careful hands.

"Look, there's Onkel Aaron," Becky exclaimed.

Sally's stomach was suddenly full of butterflies. Aaron leaned against the fence post at the end of her lane, looking as relaxed as if he intended to be there all afternoon. It didn't seem fair that he was so at ease when she felt as jittery as she had on her first day of school.

She watched him exchange greetings with the group of older kids, but he didn't move. He hadn't been waiting for them.

Lige ran ahead to go the rest of the way with his cousins, leaving her and Becky to come up to Aaron by themselves.

"Aaron. Are you waiting to walk Becky home from school?" she asked, reminding herself that she wasn't a giddy teenager any longer.

"Not Becky," he said, straightening. "It would be a pleasure, for sure, but I have other business today." He smiled at Becky, who grinned back.

"No?"

"No. I'm waiting to walk you home from school, Teacher Sally." It was said in his teasing voice, the one that had seemed lost since he'd been away. "Just like I used to."

"You never walked me home from school," she retorted, hanging on to her composure. "You let me tag along behind you and the other big boys, that's all."

"Well, then, it's time I started, ain't so?"

If he was trying to put her out of countenance, he was succeeding. She hoped she wasn't blushing.

Becky giggled. "You should carry her books, Onkel Aaron."

"I knew I was missing something." Before she could react, he'd taken her armload of books. He bent, picking up a faded duffel bag from the long grass. "Shall we go?"

He was trying to tease her, and if she reacted, he'd have succeeded. So she just nodded goodbye to Becky and started down the lane, very aware of Aaron matching steps with her.

When they'd gone a few yards she glanced back to see that Becky was skipping down the King lane, probably eager to repeat her news to the rest of the family.

She turned back to Aaron abruptly. "Enough teasing. Becky is out of sight, so you can give me my books back."

"I don't think so." He held them at arm's length, deliberately daring her to grab them.

She couldn't, because if she did, she risked touching him again. And given what had happened the last time, she wasn't about to take the chance.

"Fine. Carry them if you want to," she said. "But you should know that my sister-in-law is watching from the window."

That sobered him fast enough. He handed the books over. "Does she have binoculars or something?"

"Just a highly developed interest in everyone's affairs." She knew why now, but she couldn't say so to Aaron. Elizabeth was trying to fill up the hole in her heart where a baby should be. "She means well."

"If you say so." His voice held doubt. "Anyway, I have a good reason for being here…a first session with Star."

"Ach, that's wonderful gut." She'd wondered if he'd try to get out of it, but apparently not. "I'll have to run in the house to change my shoes and leave my books. Then I'll get Star from the barn."

She hurried on ahead to the house. Aaron was the answer to all her problems with the horse—she just knew it. Any other reasons for her pleasure in seeing him she'd push down and ignore. At least Aaron had understood why her own buggy horse was important to her, and he wouldn't let her down.

Sally raced into the house, parrying Elizabeth's questions, and hurried upstairs to change out of her school shoes and into the pair she wore in the barn. Then she ran down again, half-afraid he'd get bored and leave if she weren't quick.

No fear of that, she found when she got outside. Aaron had already brought Star out and turned him into the paddock outside the barn. When Sally reached him, he was pulling things out of the duffel bag.

"A lunge line?" she questioned. "Don't you want to harness him up?"

"Nope." He picked up a lunging halter and propped a lunge whip against the rail fence.

"But it's with the buggy that he misbehaves. What's the point of working him on the lunge line?"

Aaron planted his fists on his hips and looked at her with that frozen expression. "Did you or did you not ask me to train this animal?" He waited for her response, and she knew what it had to be.

"Okay. Yah, I asked you. You're the expert. We'll do it your way."

"Gut." He relented, his face relaxing a bit. "If I want to fix Star's problems, I have to go back to the beginning and find out where he went wrong. It might seem like a waste of time to you, but it's necessary. You understand?"

"I guess I do." Once he put it that way, she could apply the idea to what she did know about. "It's like teaching arithmetic. If a scholar gets in trouble with the advanced steps, it's usually because he or she didn't master one of the elementary ones. So we have to go back and take care of that before we can go on."

"So I'd guess you take your own time to work privately with the kid, right?"

"That's what it means to be a teacher."

Aaron seemed to study her face for a moment before he spoke. "You must be a very good teacher."

She shrugged, unaccountably embarrassed at his praise. "I guess it is like you and Star. If you care about something, you take as much time as you need to get it right, ain't so?"

"It's so." He gave her the first truly relaxed smile she'd seen from him yet, and her heart gave a deplorable flutter.

Fortunately, he didn't seem to have anything else to say, since he slipped between the rails to the paddock, intent now on the horse.

Sally held that warm moment of understanding close while she watched him. She could do it safely, because he was totally preoccupied with the gelding.

It wasn't hard to see how he'd landed in a job training horses for a living. As folks said, obviously that was what he was born to do.

Aaron talked softly to the horse as he attached the lunge line and got Star moving in a circle around him that widened slowly as he let out a little more of the line each time.

Star was skittish at first, inclined to resent the gentle taps of the lunge whip on his shoulder that kept him moving along. But after a few efforts to escape the control of the lunge line, he seemed to start paying attention. The first time he moved along properly, earning a relaxation of the shoulder taps, she wanted to cheer.

She didn't, of course. Nothing should disrupt the work that was going on. Aaron had been right at that. There was little purpose in trying to work the gelding in harness when he hadn't mastered the simplest steps.

Who had trained him initially? Whoever

it was must have taken her uncle in completely, convincing him that this was a properly trained buggy horse. She smiled, shaking her head. Simon Stoltzfus was that rare creature—an Amish man without the inborn understanding of animals. Everyone had been right to be skeptical about his unexpected gift.

Aaron was wrapped up in what he was doing, his face intent on the animal, all of his movements steady and sure. His hands—one controlling the line, the other handling the lunge whip—never wavered. When Star, tiring, attempted to bolt, Aaron seemed to know it almost before it entered the animal's head, and he let the line out a few yards before slowly drawing Star's head back around.

She'd always liked watching a person do something well, and Aaron was an expert. More, that quicksilver temper of his had been totally submerged when he worked with the horse. She'd seen others lose their tempers at signs of rebellion, but not Aaron. He just kept bringing Star back to the task at hand, never faltering.

Sally wasn't sure how long she stood there, completely captivated by the dance between man and horse. At last Star was circling the paddock at the length of the line, obedient to the guidance of the line and the sound of Aaron's voice.

Aaron brought Star into a smaller and smaller circle until the gelding stood quietly next to him, letting Aaron pat him and murmur softly, much as he had that day on the road. Then they came toward her.

Sally let go of her grip on the top railing, surprised by the indentations in her palms from the board. She must really have been concentrating not to realize how tight a grip she'd had.

"Wonderful gut," she said when they reached her. She reached out to pat Star's neck. "I can see how you got a job at a racing stable. You'd be an asset to any horse business." She hesitated. "Are they holding your place for you?"

She shouldn't have asked the question—she could see that by the way his face tightened.

"No." He cut off the word.

And cut off, too, anything else Sally might ask. For the past hour he'd been almost transformed as he'd worked with the horse, intent but open. Now that hostile, closed-down look was back on his face.

Something had gone wrong out there in the place he'd made for himself. Something that hurt him. He might think he could outrun it by coming here, but she knew better. Her own experience had taught her a hard lesson. A person couldn't just walk—or run—away from trouble. The only way to get rid of it, to keep it from eating you up, was to face it.

Aaron wouldn't do that unless he had to. Someone would have to push him into it.

Chapter Four

Aaron drew the family buggy up to the back porch the next morning in a driving rain. The wind and thunder of the previous night had passed, but the rain lingered, hard enough that Jessie hadn't wanted Becky to walk to school.

So she'd recruited him. No problem. He'd drop the kids off at the school and be on his way back, probably not even seeing Sally in passing.

It wasn't that he was avoiding her. But...

The back door rattled, and Caleb came out, standing just under the roof overhang. "Sorry," he said, his manner stiff. "Jessie shouldn't have asked you to take the kinder. I can do it."

Once again, it seemed Caleb didn't want him around the kids. What did he think Aaron was going to do? The words hovered on his tongue when Becky came running out, her schoolbooks wrapped in a plastic bag to protect them.

"I'm ready, Onkel Aaron," she sang out.

"Me, too. I don't get many chances to drive a pretty girl to school." And if Caleb didn't like it, he could be the one to make a move. "Hop on in."

But Caleb apparently didn't have anything else to say on the subject. He hoisted his daughter up the high step and into the enclosed buggy, where she settled on the back seat.

"Mammi says don't forget to stop next door," she said, obviously feeling important that she got to deliver the message.

"I won't, not with you to remind me." He clucked to the mare and she moved on a little reluctantly, no more eager to be out in the rain than anyone else. Apparently the two families shared taking the children to school in bad weather.

With Becky talking away and asking him questions, he didn't have a minute to think until after he'd picked up the youngsters at the Fisher place, including Lige, Daniel's future stepson. Once they'd all piled in, they chattered away together.

Now he had a chance to think about Caleb's reaction to his taking the children to school, and he wasn't sure he wanted to.

Did his brother think Aaron would be a bad influence on them? That becoming close to him might lead them to want to jump the fence? That seemed just plain silly, given how young they were. But what else could it be?

Irritated, he put Caleb's reactions out of his mind. Unfortunately, that seemed to leave room for Teacher Sally to slip in.

Things had turned awkward between them yesterday, and much as he'd like to blame Sally, he had to admit that he shared the fault. Face it, he was supersensitive when it came to the reason he'd left his job. The very subject made him cringe. He wasn't ready to talk about it to anyone, and he didn't know if he ever would be. Sally was just too inquisitive.

But not rude. He was the one who'd been rude, basically snubbing her when she'd asked about it.

By the time he reached the white frame schoolhouse, he'd convinced himself he ought to speak to her, at least. He ought to tell her that he wouldn't be there to work with the gelding today, anyway. Star would have to learn to behave in bad weather eventually, of course, but it was too early to take on that lesson.

So, instead of dropping the kids off, he jumped out and ran through the rain with them, spurting through the door into the vestibule that included places for wet coats and muddy boots. After wiping his shoes on the mat, Aaron opened the door into the classroom.

Instead of the orderly rows of students he expected, they all seemed to be milling around. No, that wasn't it, he realized after he watched for a moment. All of the hurrying around was purposeful, and he understood why when he found Sally struggling with the large bowl she'd pushed under a steady drip of water from the roof.

"That looks bad." He bent to help her position the bowl. "This thing will be full before you know it. Do you have a bucket?"

"Yah, two, thankfully. I sent one of the older boys to bring them from the shed. Denke, Aaron."

She stood up, looking around at the mess caused by water running in, probably since sometime in the night. Her scholars were already organized, some of them removing things from the path of the water while a couple of the older girls had set to work with mops. Apparently he didn't need to come to the rescue. Little Sally was all grown-up now, and she could take care of problems herself. The realization left him feeling oddly useless.

"I'll go outside and see if I can spot the problem." Aaron headed for the door. "It's probably a missing shingle, torn loose in that wind last night."

He ducked back out in the rain, grateful for the protection offered by the black felt Amish hat Daniel had lent him. In fact, Daniel had given him most of what he had on. The clothes he'd left behind had mostly been pitifully small on him now, and it hadn't seemed appropriate to go around in denim.

Aaron had to go around to the side to get a view of the roof, where a quick glance confirmed his suspicions. A good-sized branch had come off the black walnut tree, hitting the roof and taking several shingles with it. Fixing it would be a job for ladders and new shingles, at least.

He returned to the schoolroom to find Sally appointing a couple of the oldest boys to watch the buckets and switch them out whenever one got full.

"Yah, Teacher Sally."

"Yah, Teacher Sally."

Funny to see Sally in the teacher role, but clearly the children accepted her readily. She glanced up and met his eyes.

"How does the roof look?" She came toward him, frowning a little when she took in how wet he'd gotten.

"Nasty. A heavy branch came down on the roof and took several shingles with it. I can't tell how bad it is without going up there."

"Not now." Sally spoke to him in her teacher voice—quietly authoritative.

He found he was grinning. "Not worried about me, are you? I've been on higher roofs than that." It was worth teasing her to see the sparkle in her eyes.

"No one goes up on the schoolhouse roof in the pouring rain," she said. "Including you." She smiled suddenly. "Besides, if you did, I'd have half the boys convinced they can climb up, as well."

"I'd tell them not to." He didn't really intend to go up, knowing there was little he could do without the proper tools and equipment.

"And they'd listen about as well as you did at that age," she retorted.

Aaron realized that Becky was standing at his elbow, looking from one face to another as they spoke.

"Did you go to this school, Onkel Aaron?"

"Yah, of course I did." He pointed to one of the bigger desks in the back row. "I sat right there. And Teacher Sally was on the opposite side almost to the front."

Becky seemed to look at the schoolroom with new eyes. "So you were in school together. That's why you said about walking her home yesterday."

"We all walked to school together," Sally said. "Your daadi and your onkels, and all the kids from the Fisher farm as well as me and my brothers and sisters."

"That's a lot." Her eyes widened. "We don't have so many now."

"Your brother will be coming to school before you know it," Sally said briskly. "Now, I think it's time we got the desks back in place so we can start." She clapped her hands for attention and gave her directions.

That seemed to be the signal for him to leave. He couldn't stand here all day reminiscing.

"I'd best go, unless there's something else

I can do to help. I really came in to say we'd better skip working with Star today."

"Yah, I think you'll have gotten wet enough by then," she said. She was walking beside him to the door, and once they were inside the coatroom she paused. "One thing you can do is let Caleb know about the leak. He's on the school board, you know."

"No, I didn't know, but I'll tell him." He wasn't surprised that Caleb would have taken on that responsibility. That was his nature.

He should go, but Aaron found he was studying her face, trying to see the girl he'd known in the teacher. The voices of the children seemed far away.

"Thank you. I appreciated your help." Sally sounded breathless, and her blue eyes darkened under his steady gaze.

So. It didn't even take a touch. That spark of attraction was there even at a look. He'd better get out of range. Maybe the chilly rain would splash some common sense into him.

When the school day had ended Sally lingered, glad to have a little quiet time to clear up and get her school back the way she felt it should be. Her school. At first she hadn't been able to think of it that way, but by the end of her first year of teaching it had become hers.

Now the schoolhouse felt like a personal responsibility—her duty and her pleasure to keep it spotless and welcoming.

The water had splashed some of the books on the bottom shelf of the bookcase, and she was thankful it hadn't penetrated to the pages. She removed each volume, spreading it out carefully so the binding could dry.

Sally stroked the cover of a copy of *Anne of Green Gables*, long one of her favorite books. She'd always identified with Anne, understanding her lively personality, her vivid imagination and even her irrepressible tongue.

"A favorite book?"

She whirled at the rumble of the masculine voice. Aaron stood in the doorway, watching her with a smile.

"You startled me. I didn't expect anyone."

"Caleb sent Daniel and me to patch up the roof." He gestured toward the open door behind him, and she realized that the King wagon was pulling up to the side of the schoolhouse.

"That's kind of you." She tried to speak evenly, hoping she hadn't given away the

wave of sudden pleasure she'd felt at the sight
of him.

Aaron's lips quirked. "Daniel's the carpenter. I think he'll let me hold the ladder."

"Aaron, what's keeping you?" Daniel's call
floated into the school. "Get out here and help
me unload."

He shrugged. "Orders." He turned, and
Sally followed him as far as the doorway.

She waved at Daniel. "This is wonderful
kind of you both."

Daniel gave her his easy grin. "We can't
have our teacher getting wet, now, can we? I
told Caleb this roof needs replacing, so we'll
be setting up a work frolic soon. Maybe Saturday, yah?"

She nodded, her thoughts hurrying to what
she might have to do to get ready. "You'll tell
me what I should move and cover, ain't so?"

"I won't let him make a mess today, at
least," Aaron said. He pulled a toolbox from
the wagon bed. "Don't worry."

She retreated to the classroom and went
back to the books with a wary look at the ceil-
ing. In her experience, when men got working
on a project they sometimes didn't pay any attention to the debris they left behind. If they
were going to do a work frolic on Saturday to

replace the roof, she'd have to ask some of the mothers to help her put things away on Friday.

Working on, she listened with half her attention to the talk between Aaron and his brother. With Daniel, Aaron seemed to have established a quick, easy relationship. It was only with Caleb that she still sensed the tension between them.

As for her… Well, if she could ease his transition back to Amish life, she'd be satisfied, she told herself firmly.

It occurred to Sally that those words sounded very self-sacrificing. Were they? There might be a little self-interest in her longing to have Aaron settled here where he belonged…where she'd see him frequently.

After a bit, the hammering over her head ceased, and she heard the sounds of the ladder being taken down, and a thud as something went into the wagon. It sounded as if they were finished for the moment. She walked to the door to find Daniel coming in search of her.

"That should hold for now. Want a ride home? We can squeeze you in."

"Denke, Daniel, but I still have cleaning up to do. You'll let me know about Saturday?"

"Yah, for sure. We'll be off, then."

But when the wagon drove out, Aaron wasn't on it. He exchanged a few words with Daniel, and then he came back to the school.

"I'll help you finish."

She hesitated, wondering whether being alone in the schoolhouse was the best of ideas. But Aaron didn't wait for permission. He walked into the classroom and picked up the overflowing wastebasket.

"I see what you meant about the mess." He glanced around. "Tell me what to do."

It seemed she didn't have a choice. "If you'll pull that bookcase away from the wall, I'll see if it's wet underneath. I don't want any mold getting into the books."

"Of course not. Always with your nose in a book, that's Sally," he teased. "I remember that about you."

"That's how you learn things," she said tartly. She wasn't the little kid he could tease any longer, and he may as well start remembering it.

His suddenly serious expression caught her off balance. "You were wiser than I was, Teacher Sally. It took me years and some loneliness to find the riches in books."

It was the closest he'd come to being open about his time away, and instinct told her he'd clam up if she made too much about it. "Teacher Esther would be proud of you, no matter how long it took."

He nodded, gazing around the classroom as if seeing it as it had been years ago. "Remember how she used to read poetry to us? I could never see sense to it, until I found it on my own."

Unaccountably moved, Sally struggled for control. She didn't speak until she thought she could sound natural. "Robert Frost was always my favorite. When we have our first snow, I'll read..."

"'*Stopping By Woods on a Snowy Evening,*'" he said, smiling a little. "I know."

"Yah." She was almost afraid to let their eyes meet. It was becoming too dangerous to her peace of mind.

Maybe Aaron felt the same, because his voice changed. "When I sat back there, all I did was watch the clock."

"Or think up mischief," she added. It seemed the right moment to ask the question that troubled her. "Were you planning on leaving even then?"

"Then?" He looked startled. "No, I don't think so. I was a bit older when I started feel-

ing there was more to life than the farm and
being bossed around by Caleb."

So. She'd guessed that was at the heart of
his relationship with his big brother. She chose
her words carefully. "Caleb had a lot of responsibility thrust on him when he was very
young to handle it. I guess it's natural that
you'd clash."

He'd been gathering up discarded papers,
and his hands froze for an instant. Then he
pushed them firmly into the trash bag he held.
He finished before he let himself look at her.

"You saw a lot, little Sally."

"I keep telling you. I'm not little Sally any
longer."

"No, you're not." He studied her for a long
moment, and then he smiled. It was the full,
genuine smile she kept longing to see, and it
moved her entirely too much.

Careful, be careful. A lecture to himself
was definitely in order. He couldn't unbur-
den himself to anyone, including—no, make
that especially—Sally. A man with nothing to
give and an uncertain future might be drawn
to her warmth and sympathy, but it was entirely too dangerous.

"Well, this bag is about full." He turned

away from her smile. "I'll run it out to the trash cans. Anything else you have ready to go?"

"No, I think that's it." Sally didn't seem to notice the abrupt change in conversation. "I still have to check all the desks that were near the leak to make sure the damp didn't get into anything."

"Didn't you have your scholars check their desks?"

Her dimple returned. "Would you rely on them to be sure nothing was damp?"

"Come to think of it, I guess I wouldn't. At least if they're anything like I was at that age."

Sally was chuckling as he carted the trash bag out. That should mean she hadn't noticed anything about his reaction to her. Good. He deposited the bag in the bin and paused for a moment to scan the still-overcast sky. More rain was probably coming. Daniel's patching might well be tested.

When he got back inside, he found Sally carefully checking everything in a child's desk, touching each item. Following her lead, he started on one of the larger desks.

They worked in silence for a time. When he heard the patter of rain against the windows, he glanced up and saw Sally's look of alarm.

"A gentle rain shouldn't be a problem," he said. "I'd say leave the bucket where it is until morning, though."

She nodded. "Normally I like the sound of raindrops. But not when they're coming through the roof of my school."

"Possessive, aren't you?"

"I guess I am. I've been teaching long enough to feel as if it's mine."

"I can understand that." He glanced across the rows of desks. "Looks like you have more little ones than older scholars this year."

"Yah. It makes it difficult to hold the interest of the older ones when there are so few. But I've found they respond well when I gear their work to what they want to do after leaving school."

The intent look on her face fascinated him. More to see it again than because he was interested in educational theory, he pursued the idea.

"How do you do that? Not bringing in lessons in milking, are you?"

"Very funny." She made a face at him. "No, I stress the importance of knowing how to keep records, figure out profits and assess costs. You might be surprised at all of the book work involved nowadays. If a scholar can see how math and writing will help in his future as a farmer or small business owner, he's likely to stay interested."

He found he was looking at her with respect. "If I'd had a teacher like you, I might have paid a bit more attention in school."

"It's what I'm meant to do, I think." She hesitated. "Just as working with horses is what you're meant to do." She hurried on before he could speak. "I'm not prying about your job or why you left it. Really."

"You don't have to worry. I'm not going to bite your head off again." He frowned, not because he was angry but because he struggled for words. "I don't want to talk because it was a bad experience. It left me feeling… I don't know. Hurt, shamed, I guess. You couldn't understand." And just that much was more than he'd ever intended to say.

Sally stood very still, a book in her hands, her gaze on him. "I understand better than you know." Again she hesitated, almost as if deciding whether she wanted to trust him.

Finally she put the book down and closed the desk. "When I was nineteen, Frederick Yoder asked me to be his wife. You remember him?"

"Freddy Yoder? Isaac's little brother?"

She nodded. "I said yes. I thought… Ach, I'm not sure I thought at all. My friends were pairing off, and I thought I was in love, too. That can happen easily at that age."

If Fred Yoder had jilted her—

But she went on. "Two weeks before the wedding, I woke up and realized what I was doing. I liked Fred. I still do. But I didn't love him, and I couldn't spend the rest of my life with him."

He was swamped with sympathy for her. "You couldn't marry him if you felt that way."

"No. It wouldn't be fair to either of us." Sally took a deep breath. Obviously it still hurt to relive that time. "I told my parents, and I told Fred. It was…hard. But we canceled the plans, told everyone we'd changed our minds."

"And people gossiped. Wondered." He could see that happening. It was the reverse side of the caring in a small, close community.

She nodded. "Word got around, of course. A lot of people blamed me. Called me a flirt and worse." She shrugged, shaking her head. "I survived, thanks to my family. But when it comes to feeling hurt and shamed—yah, I know how that is."

Her voice shook a little on the last sentence. Moved, he clasped her hands in a comforting grip. Anyone would do the same, he told himself. "I'm sorry. It must have been hard for you."

"And for Fred," she added. "But he recovered." Her voice lightened. "He married Peggy Brandt, and they have twin boys now."

"And did you recover?" He studied her face, wondering how much of her pert liveliness was meant to hide her feelings.

"Of course." She said it lightly. Seeming to realize that he still held her hands, she pulled them away. "I learned a lesson. Isn't that what bad experiences are meant to do? Adults always say that. I learned not to let my head be overruled by my feelings."

If she really had learned that, he couldn't help thinking that it was a shame, because if there was ever anyone meant to love and be loved, it surely was Sally.

Chapter Five

Sally decided it was a fine thing that she didn't see much of Aaron for a couple of days. Had she totally embarrassed him, as well as herself, by telling him about Fred?

He'd been sympathetic, that was certain. She could still feel the warm grip of his hands on hers. But had he realized she was just trying to explain why she could understand his feelings? Or had he thought she was trying to draw attention to herself? Her cheeks burned at the thought.

"Sally, are you going to hand me that butter or stand there holding it until supper?" Elizabeth's tart voice brought her back to reality in a hurry.

"Sorry. I was thinking." She handed over

the butter, hoping Elizabeth was too busy to wonder what distracted her.

"It must have been something serious to have you that deep in thought. Something about the school? Or that silly horse?"

She should have known better. Elizabeth was never too busy to be curious.

"Yah, something that happened at the school." That was true enough.

"From what your brother says, they'll have that new roof on in no time on Saturday. As if he didn't have enough to do here."

Sally held her breath for a moment. "Everyone wants to help," she said, ignoring Elizabeth's tone. Did she resent the school because she had no children to go there? Somehow the revelation of Elizabeth's disappointment and pain had her thinking twice about everything she said.

"Well, I think…"

Elizabeth stopped, because Sally was already halfway to the door.

"Aaron's on his way. I have to get Star ready." She escaped before Elizabeth could point out that the horse was already in the paddock.

Was she trying to evade Elizabeth or eager to see Aaron? She pushed the question to the back of her mind for consideration later. After all, Aaron was doing her a favor by working with Star. The least she could do was help him.

She reached the paddock at the same time as Aaron. "I wasn't sure you'd come today. If you have things to do at the farm…"

"Not much." He bit off the words, frowning. "But speaking of things to do, you don't need to stay out here. I'm just going to work him on the lunge line again today, anyway."

He didn't need her, in other words. Or maybe didn't want her was closer to the truth.

"Yah, fine." She could be as snappish as he was. She swung around, but she hadn't taken more than a step before he said her name.

"Sally, wait. Sorry. I guess I got up on the wrong side of the bed today. Forgive me?"

The contrite tone made her smile. "Of course."

Not that she believed his mood had anything to do with which side of the bed he'd arisen from. Something was troubling him, but if he didn't want to tell her, she couldn't pry.

She'd learned her lesson. No more trying to get him to talk to her, but that didn't mean she'd ever stop wondering what had happened to him out there in the Englisch world.

Apparently to make up for his bad mood, Aaron talked as he put Star through his paces, explaining the steps he intended to take with the horse.

"He's responding well to voice commands," he said after an intensive twenty minutes of work. "Let's see how he reacts to the unexpected." He glanced around. "Will anyone care if you break a leafy branch off that lilac bush?"

"Not now. It'd be another story if Mamm's favorite dark purple lilacs were blooming." Seeing what he was about, Sally pulled off a long spray and took it to the paddock.

"Gut. Now when I lead him past, wave the branch off to the side."

Sally obeyed, apprehensive. Sure enough, Star reared at the sight, his eyes rolling. Aaron quieted him with voice and touch.

Catching Sally's expression, he smiled. "He'll do much better with blinders on. I just wanted to see if that side view was what set him off."

They went on to take turns leading Star past a variety of objects. Once he'd settled down, Aaron led him out of the paddock and over to where the buggies were parked, talking casually.

Star stopped, his ears pricking forward, but then he responded to that low, steady voice and walked on. Sally, following, decided it was not too surprising. If Aaron spoke to her in that warm, soft tone, she'd probably do the same.

When they'd circled all the buggies several times, Aaron stopped, letting the rope go slack. Star, apparently deciding he was done, dropped his head and began cropping the grass.

"That'll do for today." Aaron patted the gelding on the shoulder, but his gaze was on Sally. "He's coming along better than I feared. Next time we'll try working him with parts of the harness on. After school all right?"

"I can't be here then." She felt a sharp pang of regret. "Some of the women are coming to help me cover everything in the schoolhouse to prepare for the roof project the next day."

"You don't trust us not to make a mess, in other words." He gave her his rare smile. "You're probably wise. Okay if I work Star anyway?"

"Yah, for sure." She swallowed disappointment. She hadn't realized how much she'd been looking forward to these sessions. Well, there was nothing wrong with that, was there? It was natural to want to spend time with an old friend after all these years.

She was still telling herself that when she waved goodbye to Aaron and headed back to the house and paused to wash her hands at the outside sink. Elizabeth wouldn't want hands smelling like horse in her kitchen.

Elizabeth was setting the table for supper, and she hurried to take the plates.

"I'll take care of that, Elizabeth. I haven't been around much to help you lately."

"You have your work to keep you busy." Elizabeth's normally ruddy face grew a bit redder. "But spending so much time with Aaron King—that's not your job, and it certain sure isn't a gut idea."

Sally counted to five before she spoke. "Aaron is training Star for me without charging. The least I can do is help him, ain't so?"

"Ach, Sally, don't you see what's happening to you? You're always so sensible about men since what happened with Fred, but you flew out of here like a bird when you saw Aaron coming. Don't bother to tell me you're not attracted to him, because I wouldn't believe it."

Only the fact that there was genuine concern behind Elizabeth's sharp voice kept Sally from flaring out at her. This time she counted to ten.

"Aaron is an old friend. If I can do something to ease his way back into Amish life, I should do it."

"What makes you think he wants back into Amish life?" Elizabeth planted her hands on her hips. "He ran away before because he wanted the excitement out in the world. What happens when he starts wanting excitement again?"

"Maybe he won't."

"And maybe he will. You spending time with Aaron is just going to make folks talk. If you don't care about that, your brother and I have to, or what would your mamm and daad say?" Her face softened in time to avert an explosion on Sally's part. "Think about it, Sally. And then about how you'd feel if you gave your heart to him and he went away again."

"That's nonsense." She couldn't listen to any more. "I'm not going to give my heart to anyone. I'm not that foolish, no matter what you think."

Brave words. A month ago she'd have meant them. Unfortunately, she wasn't sure they were true any longer.

* * *

Every family in the church district naturally wanted to participate in putting the new roof on their school. Aaron and his brothers and Zeb managed to be the first to arrive on Saturday morning, but a steady stream of wagons and buggies pulled in behind them.

Aaron glanced over the line of buggies. "Almost looks like a church Sunday. We'll have plenty of helpers."

"For sure. We'll get it done in no time." Daniel grinned. "We have enough help that Onkel Zeb doesn't need to go up on the roof."

Zeb gave him a mock glare. "Don't you go saying I'm old, Daniel King. I can work as well as the next man."

"You can, but give the younger guys a chance. They need to show off for their wives and girlfriends, you know."

Aaron slid down from the wagon and led the buggy horse to the improvised hitching post. A buggy pulled in right next to him, and in moments, the normally quiet school was a hive of activity. Ezra Brandt, who claimed to have raised more barns than any man in the county, took charge of organizing the workers and materials.

It wasn't long before Aaron had his assignment. He grabbed a pry bar and started up the ladder behind Daniel. If he hung out with his brother the carpenter, he shouldn't make any foolish mistakes.

Removing the old roof was the first order of business. Shreds of shingles and tar paper began to fly, and Aaron knew Sally had been right to anticipate a mess. Still, no one would leave the site until the school was ready for business again on Monday.

"Done any roofing work while you were away?" Daniel pulled off a long strip of tar paper.

"Nothing like this." He put his back into pulling out a stubborn nail. "I did a little mending now and then when it was needed. Most of the guys would pitch in wherever something had to be done, although some of them didn't know one end of a hammer from the other."

"I trust you showed them." Caleb, working on the other side of him, surprised him by joining the conversation.

"I tried." Aaron shrugged. "Seems like growing up on a farm means you learn how to do a lot of things. I took it for granted that everyone does, too, but they don't."

"They must know horses, if they worked for a stable," Daniel said.

"Most of them had some experience," Aaron admitted. "If they didn't, the boss figured that out fast and got rid of them. But they weren't what I'd call handy."

"I'm glad to know you found some benefit from working on the farm."

He wasn't sure if there was sarcasm in Caleb's comment or not. Remembering what Sally had said about him, Aaron decided to give him the benefit of the doubt.

"That wasn't the only good thing," he said mildly.

The three of them worked in silence for a time, side by side. It was a surprisingly comfortable silence.

Aaron glanced down at the schoolyard. Onkel Zeb was supervising a group of boys who were hauling the debris away and stacking it, while the women and girls were already organizing lunch.

"Seriously, how did you convince Onkel Zeb not to climb up on the roof?" he asked.

Caleb shook his head. "I didn't. That was Jessie. She persuaded him that he was needed more down there."

"He never turns Jessie down," Daniel added. "I think she could ask him anything."

"Yah." Caleb sent a worried glance down at the group of women. "I wish I could have talked her into not coming today, but she was set on being here."

"I'd guess the other women won't let her do too much." Aaron thought that was as close as he should come to mention Jessie's obvious pregnancy.

Caleb nodded, maybe finding comfort in the thought.

The three of them moved to another row of shingles, working steadily. Aaron listened to the flow of Pennsylvania Dutch, punctuated by frequent laughter. There was a reason they called it a work frolic—the Amish found enjoyment in doing a project like this together. He'd forgotten.

It wasn't that folks in the outside world didn't get together to do good things. The boss had organized a crew to work on a Habitat for Humanity house just last year, and most of the guys had contributed their time. Enjoyed it, too.

But that had been something special in their lives. This was routine. If a job needed to be done, the community didn't wait to be asked. They just came together and did it.

Aaron stretched, looking around, surprised by how much they'd accomplished already.

"We're almost ready to start putting the new roof on," he said. "That's fast."

Daniel looked up with his ready smile. "You should have seen us when we raised a barn for Sam Fisher. Now, that was a big project, and it was ready for use by sundown."

Aaron looked suitably impressed. "I noticed the new barn. What happened to the old one?"

"Fire," Caleb said shortly.

"That was when Caleb had his accident," Daniel added.

"Not my favorite memory," Caleb grumbled.

"If you hadn't broken your leg, Jessie wouldn't have come to mind the kinder. And you wouldn't be happily married now," Daniel said. "I'd guess that's worth a broken leg."

"Onkel Zeb said it was God's plan working out." Caleb stopped working for a moment, his expression considering. "I thought maybe He could have found a less painful way."

"Not a chance. You're so stubborn it's a wonder the gut Lord didn't hit you with a two-by-four," Daniel said.

Aaron decided he'd have to give that idea some thought. In spite of Caleb's grumbling, Aaron knew he'd take a broken leg in a second to have his Jessie.

Maybe God had some plan in mind that included the painful things that had happened to him, Aaron thought. But he'd just as soon decide his future for himself. Wouldn't he?

He edged away from that thought, looking across the group gathered in the schoolyard again. His gaze snagged on Sally. She was bending over Jessie, helping her into a chair she'd brought out from the schoolroom. Caring…that was typical of Sally.

Even as he thought it, Sally looked up as if she'd heard his thought. Her gaze seemed to be drawn to his. Even across the distance between them, he felt its impact.

She turned away to say something to Jessie, so quickly that he felt he might have imagined that moment. He turned resolutely back to the work.

When the men started to come down the ladders, the flow of activity around the tables reached fever pitch. Sally, keeping a wary eye on Jessie, saw neighbor Leah Fisher intercept

Jessie when she attempted to pick up a tray. Arm around Jessie, Leah steered her away.

Relieved, Sally grabbed a tray laden with sandwiches and headed for the picnic tables. Obviously other people besides her had noticed how tired Jessie looked. Her thoughts flew to the midwife, and she hoped Jessie's household of men had sense enough to call at the right time.

As she circulated around the tables, Sally made an attempt to speak to everyone, thanking each person for helping out today. Most of them turned her thanks away with a joke or a laugh, but she wouldn't want anyone to think she didn't appreciate their efforts. The school gained its strength from the willing support of the community, and she'd never want that to change.

The King family was sitting at one end of a picnic table—at least the male part of it was. Becky, looking solemn and self-conscious, was carrying away used dishes.

Timothy and Lige, his soon-to-be cousin, seemed equally impressed to be eating with the workers. Sally paused to tap each one on his hat, earning a quick grin from Timothy and a shy smile from Lige.

"I saw how hard you two were working. Onkel Zeb kept you busy, ain't so?"

Zeb, sitting next to the boys, gave them a fond look. "They are gut workers, both of them. I'm fortunate to have two such strong helpers."

Timothy swelled with importance at the words. "We are strong, Teacher Sally. Look at the big pile we made of the shingles and tar paper." He pointed a small finger at the stack of debris, situated so that it could easily be loaded onto a wagon and hauled away.

"That's very impressive. And we'll be sehr glad not to worry about the rain getting into the schoolroom when you're done."

"Yah, we don't want our teacher getting wet," Daniel said, reaching across to rest his hand for a moment on Lige's shoulder.

"Or our scholars missing any class time," Caleb added. "Hope you didn't lose anything important to the water, Teacher Sally."

"Nothing that can't be replaced," she said. "At least the books have dried out without damage."

"We all know how important the books are to the teacher." Aaron's smile seemed to warm her. "She treasures those more than anything."

"Some of us learn to love reading early," she retorted. "And others are late bloomers."

"What's a late bloomer?" Timothy asked.

Caleb chuckled. "I think she means that your onkel Aaron never read anything he didn't have to when he was in school."

Timothy fixed wide blue eyes on Aaron. "But you have some books in your room. I saw them."

"That's right." Aaron actually looked a little embarrassed. "It took me some growing up to learn how much books had to offer me. You'll be better off if you learn to like reading early."

"Mammi reads to us every night," he said. "I'll like learning to read, but…" A trace of dismay crossed his face.

Sally patted him, understanding. "Mammi will still read to you at night, even after you can read for yourself. You don't have to worry about that."

"That's right," Caleb said. "Teacher Sally has the right of it. Mammi loves to read to you."

"Yah." Timothy's face cleared. "She does."

Sally couldn't help glancing at Aaron. He was watching her with Timothy, and his expression was so tender that it made her breath catch. He might not be ready to admit it, but everything he wanted was right here with his family. Whether it included her or not.

She straightened, realizing that Daniel was elbowing Caleb. Oops. She wasn't sure how much they'd noticed, but if she wanted to avoid people talking about her, she'd have to start being careful now.

"I'd best get back to work," she said, giving the kinder a smile. "Everyone needs a hearty lunch in order to finish the roof."

Moving away, she tried not to look at Aaron. She was being foolish, reading so much into every glance. She'd do better to focus on things she could do something about, like taking the desserts around.

A half hour later, most folks had finished eating, and there was a gradual movement back to the work area. Apparently, they were ready to start putting the new roofing in place. It looked as if they'd be finished in time for her and her volunteers to do some cleaning up inside. She'd have to put in as much work as possible today, since tomorrow was the Sabbath.

She'd avoided looking inside the schoolhouse thus far, but finally she just had to take a peek. Standing in the doorway, all she could do was shake her head. Thankfully they'd covered everything, because the tarps and the floor were littered with scraps of tar paper, shingles and the dust that must have been accumulating for a few years.

"I see what you mean about a mess." Aaron's voice, so close behind her, startled her. She swung around to find him inches away.

"I didn't hear you." Sally tried for a natural tone, but the words had come out sounding oddly breathless. "Did…does someone want me?"

Aaron's eyes twinkled. "Probably. But I thought you might want to know how I made out with Star yesterday."

"Oh. Yes, of course." She eased backward a step so she could breathe. "Elizabeth said you'd been there working. How did Star react to the harness?"

He still had an amused look in his eyes, as if he knew full well why she'd backed up. "Better than I thought. He's been harnessed before, so he worked pretty well. He didn't like it when I put the blinders on, though."

"No. He did a lot of head tossing when I tried it."

"A good sign he needs them. He's too distracted by what he sees in his peripheral vision. I worked him for about fifteen minutes on the lunge line with them. He settled down eventually. I'll work him a bit more that way, and then we can try ground-driving him."

She nodded. *We*, he'd said. It sounded as if she'd get to participate. "Sounds gut. Tomorrow's Sunday, so Monday?"

"Yah, I guess." Something wary had crossed his face at the mention of the Sabbath.

Sally hesitated for a moment, but she couldn't seem to help one little question. "Will you be going to worship tomorrow?"

He nodded. "I have to, don't I? I can't be here and stay away."

"You don't need to brace yourself as if it's going to be a battle," she said. "I'm sure everyone will wilkom you."

"Everyone? You really think so?" He sounded skeptical. "I'd guess there will be a few who aren't so eager to see the bad boy back."

"Nonsense." The fear that he might be right gave extra emphasis to her voice. "Nobody would…" The rest of the sentence faded as she saw Elizabeth standing on the porch behind Aaron.

"Sally. We could use your help." She divided a disapproving look between the two of them. It looked as if Sally were in for a lecture.

A wave of defiance swept through her, startling her. She wasn't doing anything wrong, and she wouldn't let anyone make her feel guilty.

Head held high, she marched out of the schoolroom.

Chapter Six

Aaron's stomach lurched as Caleb turned the buggy into the lane of the Miller farm, and it wasn't because of the sharp turn. He was on his way to worship for the first time in more years than he wanted to think about.

As they drove up the lane toward the barn, he saw the lineup of buggies parked along one side of the barn. One after another they stood there, a visible symbol of the Amish at worship. Horses and buggies… Onkel Zeb always said that was one of the things that kept the community together. He hadn't had much time for that idea when he'd been a teenager, longing to be behind the wheel of a car.

As soon as Caleb pulled up near the wide door to the barn, two teenage boys, probably Josh Miller's kids, came running to take the buggy and park it. They'd take care of the horses, as well. The kids in the host family always had plenty to do on worship Sunday. Aaron caught a curious look directed at him, and he figured he'd better brace himself for plenty more.

Sally had been naive when she'd snapped at him on that subject. Or else she was just so tenderhearted herself that she couldn't imagine others wouldn't be as welcoming as she was. But he didn't have any illusions.

The curiosity would be bad enough. He'd be surprised if he didn't encounter outright hostility. Probably a few people had thought "good riddance" when they'd heard he was gone. He'd had a reputation as a teen, and careful families hadn't wanted their daughters anywhere near him.

None of his family seemed to be talking much, making him wonder if they were apprehensive about what was to come. Still, usually folks were fairly quiet when they gathered for worship, as he recalled. Afterward, during lunch, there'd be time for visiting and catching up on all the news.

He followed his brothers and his uncle to the line that was forming along one side of the barn door. Onkel Zeb first, then Caleb holding Timothy by the hand, Daniel, and he brought up the rear. Jessie moved slowly to the line of women along the opposite side, with Becky skipping at her side. Jessie murmured something to her, and Becky slowed to a sedate walk.

Before he'd had a chance to look for familiar faces among the men, their line had begun to move. He was carried forward, taken inexorably along with the others to their seats on the men's side of the rows of benches ready for them. The routine of preparing for worship was as settled as the worship service itself.

The animals had been moved out, and the barn was as spotless as a barn could possibly be. He hated to think of the amount of work that involved. Most folks were glad they didn't have to host worship more than once a year.

He sat, trying to look at ease while he took surreptitious glances along the rows of faces. There was Amos Burkhalter, who'd been his closest friend in his class at school. He sat at the end of the row in front of them, with four little boys arranged next to him like a series of steps.

Was it actually possible that Amos, who'd been as prone to trouble as he'd been, was the father of all those kids? Who had been brave enough to take him on? He'd have to find out after the service.

The two ministers filed in and took their places, followed by Bishop Thomas Braun. Aaron had thought him old when he'd left, but he didn't look any different now. A few more gray hairs in his beard, maybe. Their gazes crossed, and Aaron looked at the floor quickly. He'd have to encounter the bishop sometime, he supposed, but he wasn't eager for the meeting.

The song leader started the long notes of the first hymn, and Daniel stuck a hymnbook into his hands. Actually he remembered the words, but Daniel wasn't taking any chances.

The long, slow cadence of the hymns was oddly comforting. They seemed to settle his mind. He took advantage of the moment to risk a sidelong look at the women's section. Becky was snuggled close to Jessie, and Leah Fisher sat on Jessie's other side. A row ahead of them he spotted Sally, realizing he'd know the back of her neck and her glossy hair under the sedate kapp no matter where she was.

Now, what was Sally doing sitting in the row with the young married women? She ought, by rights, to be with the unmarried girls.

Was this a tacit statement that she considered herself a maidal, an old maid? The anger he felt at the thought surprised him. Sally shouldn't put thoughts of marriage away just because she'd made a mistake once.

He mulled that over as the service moved on, finding no answers. Sally would be a wonderful wife to someone who deserved her. Not him, of course, but someone who would bring a spotless reputation and a heart of devotion.

The bishop began to speak. Aaron, prepared to sleep with his eyes open, found he was listening in spite of himself. He'd been half-afraid the sermon might be on the subject of the prodigal's return, but Bishop Thomas made no reference to him. Good. He didn't need or want to be the object of everyone's attention. There'd be enough of that after worship.

By the time the service had wound to its conclusion, Aaron found that one leg had gone to sleep. He'd lost the knack of sitting through a three-hour worship service, apparently. Timothy, leaning against Caleb, had slept through the last hour, but he woke when his father moved.

In a moment the barn was bustling with activity. The women and girls went out, most to help with the lunch, he guessed. The men, including his brothers, started to work immediately, turning the benches into the tables and benches they'd need for the meal.

He wasn't sure who had invented the convertible tables, but it had been a clever idea. Later they'd be folded up and loaded onto the church wagon, ready to be moved to the next site of worship in two weeks' time.

Once lunch started, folks settled down to talk, catching up on all that had happened since they'd been together. He managed to touch base with Amos, and returned to Onkel Zeb afterward, grinning.

"You found a friend, yah?" Zeb said. "Do you think Amos much changed?"

"He's turned into a pillar of the church, it seems. I don't know how Mary Ann did it. But he's about to get his comeuppance, because those boys of his look as ripe for mischief as he ever was."

His uncle chuckled. "That's always the way. Kinder repeat their parents' deeds. The only hope for a parent is that you'll live long enough to see their kinder do the same to them."

Sally swept past them just then, clearly on her way to the kitchen with a tray. She gave him a nod and kept moving.

What had Elizabeth said to her after she'd found them together in the schoolhouse yesterday? Nothing pleasant, he could be sure. Elizabeth didn't approve of him.

That was okay, because he didn't approve of himself. And if everyone knew what he'd been accused of and why he'd left the Englisch, plenty more would disapprove. He turned, not wanting to be caught staring after Sally, and found the bishop bearing down on him.

Onkel Zeb slipped away, obviously thinking he ought to give them privacy. At the moment, Aaron would rather have protection. A flare of panic struck. What was Bishop Thomas going to say?

People around them drifted away or began loud conversations with each other, obviously following Zeb's lead.

"Aaron." The bishop surveyed him for a moment, and then clapped him on the shoulder, smiling. "It's wonderful gut to see you home again. It's been a long time."

"It has, I know." He took a breath. May as well be honest. "The family would have been disappointed if I hadn't come to worship with them, but I wasn't sure others would feel that way."

"Ach, that's foolishness." His grip tightened

strongly, reminding Aaron that in addition to being the bishop, he was also the wheelwright, and he had muscles like iron. "The Leit will always wilkom those who come back to us with an open and contrite heart."

Aaron was at a loss for words. His heart felt like a chunk of rock. He didn't think the bishop would consider that either open or contrite.

"Take your time." Maybe Bishop Thomas saw that he wasn't ready yet. "When you feel like talking to me, you know where I am."

He moved off, leaving Aaron still speechless. Coming back the way the bishop saw it meant confession—meant telling everything, including the reason he'd come back. It meant kneeling in front of the whole congregation and asking to return…to return forever.

He didn't see his way clear to doing any of that. If he couldn't even be open with Sally… But what was he thinking? Of course he couldn't say anything to Sally. She was little more than a kid, and he certainly couldn't burden her with his story. Maybe the best thing he could do for everyone was to walk away again.

Someone touched his arm, and he jerked around. Sally.

"Don't be alarmed," she said quickly, her voice low. "Can you find Caleb for Jessie? There's nothing wrong, but she's tired and needs to go home. We'll be in the kitchen."

He nodded a quick assent, everything else forgotten. Was the baby about to arrive?

Sally hurried back to the kitchen, trying to reassure herself. Everything was fine. Aaron would find Caleb, and he'd take charge of getting his family home.

Jessie sat at the kitchen table where she'd left her, leaning her head on her hand. Becky stood nearby, looking scared.

Sally bent over Jessie, touching her shoulder gently. "I didn't see Caleb, so I sent Aaron to look for him. Don't worry. He'll be here soon."

"I'm all right." Jessie looked up and tried to smile. "Silly of me, but I just felt like I wanted to go home."

"And so you will. In the meantime, if you want to lie down in one of the bedrooms…"

"No, no." She looked horrified at the thought. "I'll just sit here."

She didn't want to draw attention to herself, of course. "Well, it looks as if Mary Miller left everything ready for tea. Shall I make you a cup?"

"That sounds gut." Jessie held her hand out to Becky, who came and gave her a cautious hug. "Maybe a weak cup of tea with sugar for Becky, too. I'm afraid I scared her when I started feeling dizzy."

"I'm not scared, Mammi," Becky said, belying the look in her eyes. "I was just worried." She kept her arm around Jessie's shoulders.

"Two cups of tea coming right up." Sally turned the gas on under the teakettle and took two cups from the tray that was ready. It was sweet to see Becky so attached to her stepmother. She hadn't had much mothering from her own mammi, but Jessie's warm heart was more than filling that gap.

Mary had the water already hot, and it only took a minute to bring it back to boiling. Sally took a quick look out the back window. The women still sat around the tables, having dessert and talking. That was just as well. She didn't think Jessie wanted a lot of people fussing over her.

Still, Jessie could have done better than Sally. Once again she had the sense that she was in over her head. Carrying the cups to the table, she set them in front of Jessie and Becky. Jessie immediately wrapped her fingers around the cup and drank thirstily.

Was tea a good idea if she were going into labor? Sally had no notion, but it seemed to calm Jessie. She smiled, patting Becky.

"Drink up. Your daadi will be here in a minute."

Sally perched on the edge of her chair, not wanting to be too obviously watching for the men. What was taking so long? Most likely, Caleb had walked off to have a look at the Burkhalters' orchard, or their corn crop, or something equally fascinating to him.

Even as she thought that, she saw Caleb and Aaron heading for the porch at a fast walk. At least they had sense enough not to run and get everyone upset. Caleb did run once he got inside, brushing past Sally as if she weren't there to get to his wife.

He bent over her, murmuring softly to her. Aaron paused next to Sally, his hand brushing her arm. "Is she all right?"

"I think so. She felt a little dizzy, but she says she just wants to go home."

He nodded. "Onkel Zeb and Daniel went to hitch up the buggy. They'll be along any minute now." He gave her a curious glance. "How did you get involved?"

"Becky was frightened, so she ran and got me." She wrinkled her nose. "I guess she thinks teachers can solve anything, but in this case…"

"It looks to me as if you did fine." He squeezed her arm in a quick gesture. "Here comes the buggy. Jessie, shall we carry you out?"

"Ach, no, how silly." Jessie's voice was stronger, and her color was better now that Caleb's arm was around her. "I'm just tired, that's all."

"Are you sure?" Caleb helped her up. "Maybe the midwife—"

"No, not yet." Her voice was firm, and she walked across the kitchen without hesitation. "Denke, Sally."

"Yah, denke," Caleb repeated.

Aaron held the door, and they all went to the buggy where Daniel waited with Onkel Zeb and Timothy. Jessie clearly wanted to get away without causing comment, but folks were bound to notice that they were leaving early.

And ask questions. Once the buggy had pulled out, Sally found herself surrounded. It hadn't occurred to her that she'd be the one they questioned, and she had her work cut out for her parrying all the concerned inquiries.

Before long most people were soon ready

to pack up and head for home, while a small group stayed to help clean up and prepare for the young people's singing that evening.

By the time Sally was back in the buggy with Ben and Elizabeth, she was ready for Elizabeth's questions. She repeated all the answers she'd already given.

"I wonder if the boppli..." Elizabeth broke off suddenly. Sally met her gaze and grinned. They were both thinking the same thing. Elizabeth shot a glance at Ben, who was studiously looking elsewhere.

"I guess we'll know soon enough," Sally said. "Especially if we see Anna Miller's buggy coming."

Elizabeth nodded. At least she wasn't carrying on about how unsuitable it was for Sally to be involved. "I wonder..." she began, but her words were cut off when Ben pulled up suddenly.

A car was tipped down over the bank on the right side of the road, up against a utility pole, which tilted at a dangerous angle. Fortunately, the lines it carried were off the road. The driver, a young man who looked to be in his twenties, stood surveying the wreck.

Ben hailed him. "Are you hurt? Can we do anything to help?"

The man scrambled up the bank to the buggy. "Thanks, but I'm okay. I swerved to miss a deer. It's fine, but my car's a mess."

"If we can give you a lift, we will be happy to."

He shook his head. "I already called to report it. But thanks." He stood back, waving as Ben clicked to the horse and they moved off.

Elizabeth glanced back at him. "I hope he's really all right. I wouldn't want to run into something in a car. And young people always drive too fast."

Ben exchanged glances with Sally. "No need to worry. When Frank Williams drives us places, he always goes ten miles slower than the speed limit."

Sally hid a smile. Elizabeth was a born worrier, it seemed. At least the car accident had diverted her attention from Jessie, so hopefully she wouldn't run over there filled with questions and concerns.

"We'd best get home and get ready to leave for your sister's place," Ben said. "Sally, you know they'd be happy to see you if you want to come."

"That's right," Elizabeth echoed.

"I appreciate it, but I have a book I want to read for school this afternoon."

Ben and Elizabeth planned to visit her sister and family this afternoon and stay for supper. It was kind of them to invite her, but the thought of an afternoon on her own was too tempting. Besides, she knew how much Elizabeth looked forward to visiting with her sister. They'd do much better without her.

When Ben and Elizabeth had driven off, Sally settled herself in the living room rocker with a book. She liked to read to her scholars each day after the lunch recess, but it could be a challenge to find something that would interest all ages.

She found it difficult to focus, and she knew why. Aaron had just spoken with the bishop when she'd approached him earlier, and the look on Aaron's face had startled her. He had looked like a man who found himself trapped and was searching for a way out.

But Bishop Thomas hadn't looked stern or forbidding to her—he'd given Aaron a clap on the shoulder in his usual friendly way. Still, something about his words had upset Aaron. If it hadn't been for the necessity of finding Caleb quickly, she'd have tried to find out. Not that Aaron would have been likely to confide.

Sally glanced toward the King farm, wondering about Jessie, and saw a buggy being driven at a fast trot toward her. Dropping the book, she hurried through the house to the back door. Jessie?

Aaron had already flung himself from the buggy when she reached him and was racing for the phone shanty.

"Our phone is out. Does yours work?"

"I don't know." She hurried after him. "Is it Jessie?"

He was already picking up the receiver. Then he slammed it down again. "Dead."

"It must have been the accident. You would have gone past before it happened. A car in the ditch, and the pole knocked sideways. Jessie?"

"She's in labor. I don't know what's wrong, but she wants the midwife right away. Daniel ran to get Leah, and I said I'd call."

She could see the scrap of paper he clutched—presumably Anna's phone number. Sally tried to think what the best possibility would be. The midwife lived even farther out the same road, and her phone might well be affected, too.

"You'll have to go for her," she said. "That's the quickest thing."

"It would be, if I knew where she lived. You forget I've been away a long time."

"No problem." She was already hurrying to the buggy. "I'll go with you."

He hesitated for a moment, as if trying to come up with another option. Then he pulled himself up with an easy motion and grabbed the lines. They were already heading back down the lane before it occurred to Sally that perhaps she should have left a note for Ben and Elizabeth.

It was too late now, and most likely she'd be home long before they got back. Anna's clinic wasn't that far off, but just far enough that she was in another church district.

"I hope she's home." Aaron sent a worried look back over his shoulder. "If we can't find her… Maybe I should have headed toward town and tried to get the ambulance."

"If Jessie asked for the midwife, then that's what she needs." She prayed she was right. "Anna would leave a note on the door if she went anywhere, and chances are she'll be at home with the family."

Anna had taken over the midwife practice that her mother-in-law had run for so long.

Initially there had been those who'd said she was too young, but Anna had proved herself.

Aaron still looked worried. Sally reached out to pat his arm. "It will be all right. You'll see. Leah can handle things until we get back with the midwife."

"I hope you're right," he muttered. "I'd rather have heard about the baby when it was all over."

"You don't mean that. I know you don't. It's a blessing to be able to help at such a time."

"Is it?" He gave her as much of a smile as he could probably manage right now. "You're a nice person, Sally."

She shook her head impatiently. "Anyone would rush to help. I care about Jessie. And so do you."

Aaron's face tightened. "I guess I do. That's the trouble with coming home. It won't be easy to go away again."

Sally's heart seemed to stop for a second. "Are you planning to go away, Aaron?"

"I don't know." His jaw clamped, and his face was suddenly forbidding. "I don't know," he repeated.

Sally clasped the edge of the seat with her

fingers, trying to deny the pain she felt. But she couldn't. If Aaron left, she was afraid he'd be taking her heart with him.

Chapter Seven

Aaron's nerves were jangling by the time they neared the farm, the midwife sitting between him and Sally in the buggy. Anna was everything, he supposed, that one would want a midwife to be, with a calm, capable manner and a warm, sweet smile. She seemed to radiate confidence. He wished he felt the same.

Sally and the midwife had been chatting during the ride, but as he neared the lane, Sally leaned forward. "Just drop me here, Aaron. You'll want to get Anna straight to Jessie."

Any other time he might have argued, but he couldn't think of anything else until he'd fulfilled his duty. If only the phones...

He pulled up long enough for Sally to jump down. "Let me know if I can do anything to help," she said.

Aaron turned toward the house, wondering how long it had been. He'd gone as fast as he could, hadn't he?

"I'm sure I'll be in time," Anna said, as if she'd read his thoughts. "First babies always take a while to arrive."

"I hope so, or I wouldn't want to face my brother. Caleb is probably twice as nervous as I am."

"I haven't lost a father yet," she said lightly. He supposed she meant it to be reassuring, but it didn't help him, and he didn't think it would Caleb either.

They came to a stop at the porch, and he hopped down, ground tying the horse. Time enough to unharness once he knew how things were with Jessie.

He followed Anna inside. Caleb was there to meet them, looking as if he'd been dragged through a knothole. He clasped Anna's hands.

"She's upstairs. Leah is with her. I'll show you—"

Anna shook her head. "I'm sure I can find them." Her smile seemed to include all of them. "If I need anything, I'll call you."

As soon as she left the room, Caleb turned on Aaron. "What took so long? It shouldn't have taken you an hour."

He'd snap back, but he could see the worry etched in his brother's face. "All the phones along the road are out. There was a car accident. So I had to go for the midwife."

"An accident? I hope it wasn't bad," Onkel Zeb said, looking up from saying something to the kinder.

"I don't think so. Sally says they passed it on their way home from church. Must have happened not long after we came home."

They heard footsteps. Leah came down the stairs. "It's all right," she said quickly. "Caleb, Anna says you can go up and see Jessie for a few minutes." She caught his arm when he brushed past her, and smiled. "Be calm. Be loving. Don't upset her or we won't let you in again."

"Yah. Right." He hurried off.

Leah looked after him for a moment and then headed for the stove. "Is there coffee hot?"

"Yah, for sure." Zeb seemed to collect himself. "And some sticky buns that Jessie made yesterday. Sit and relax a bit."

"It will be wilkom." She sat at the table with the kinder. "Rebecca is coming over in a bit with supper." She looked from the young ones to the adults with an expression that said she found the grown-ups lacking. "Daniel, isn't there something you and the kinder could be doing outside?"

Galvanized, Daniel got up. "The chickens. We've gotten all behind today, ain't so? Let's go gather the eggs and see to the food and water."

Becky hesitated, looking at Leah. "Can't I see Mammi? I could help."

"I know you're a wonderful gut helper." Leah smoothed back her hair. "Mammi will need you later, after this boppli comes, ain't so?"

Becky didn't look entirely satisfied, but she nodded and left with Daniel and her brother. Leah divided a disapproving look between Zeb and Aaron.

"If you two want to be helpful, you'll keep the kinder occupied so they don't worry."

"I wasn't here," Aaron protested. "I went for the midwife."

"You're right," Zeb said, setting a sticky bun in front of her. "I should have thought." He gave her a rueful glance. "But Caleb has been enough to handle."

Leah sipped her coffee. "I'm sure. Well, you try to keep him busy when he comes back down. Worrying never helped anyone, and

Jessie is in gut hands, and everything is going as it should."

"We'll try." Zeb patted her shoulder. "You're a gut friend, Leah."

"Ach, it's what she would do for me." Leah drained her cup and set it in the sink. "I'll go up and chase Caleb down now. Ben and the older boys will be over to help with the milking and anything else you need."

Zeb nodded, accepting it as normal. Aaron turned it over in his mind. Neighbors helped each other in a crisis out there in the world, he was sure, but they seemed to wait to be asked. The Amish were such a part of each other's lives that they didn't need to wait. They'd just be there.

The afternoon wore on. It proved impossible to get Caleb out of the house, so they stopped trying. Deciding to leave him to Zeb, Aaron got up.

"I'll go out and see that everything is ready for the milking."

"You don't have to do that." Caleb's reply seemed almost automatic by now, and Aaron's patience finally snapped.

"If you don't trust me to do it, just say so."

Their gazes met, and for a long moment, he and his brother stared at each other. Then

Caleb shook his head. "I thought... I was too hard on you before. Expecting you to do a man's work when you were just a boy. I see that now. I don't want to push you away again."

All of Aaron's preconceptions about Caleb crumbled into dust. "It's not... That's not why I went. Well, not the whole reason, anyway. It wasn't your doing—it was mine. Now that I'm here..." He paused, trying to get it clear in his own mind. "I just want you to treat me like your brother."

The kitchen was so silent they could hear the soft movements from the room over their heads. Caleb's face contorted. Then he grabbed Aaron in a rough hug, shaking him a little. When he drew back, Aaron thought he saw unshed tears in his eyes. He knew there were in his.

"Yah," Caleb said finally. "Get along out to the milking shed. There's work to do."

Grinning, Aaron went.

Aaron stayed busy outside for well over an hour, but by the time he and Daniel returned to the house, he was wondering what they'd find. If the baby hadn't come yet, he'd think it was time to start worrying.

They found Rebecca, Daniel's intended, in

control in the kitchen. Caleb was pacing from one end of the room to the other and then back again. Aaron had heard all the jokes about expectant fathers, but he'd never actually expected to see his controlled oldest brother in such a state.

Caleb swung on them. "Is the phone working yet? I think—"

"Hush." Rebecca had paused, one hand on the oven door, seeming to listen to something above them.

And then they all heard it—the thin, protesting wail of the newborn.

There was a concerted rush to the hallway. Caleb had his foot on the first step when Leah came out of the room. "Jessie is fine," she said quickly. She smiled. "You have a son."

"Praise the gut Lord," Zeb said, his face seeming ready to split with his smile. He pounded Caleb on the back. "A new baby. A little bruder for Becky and Timothy."

"I'll show him how to play with my blocks," Timothy said, squirming toward the stairs.

"He won't be ready for that for a long time," Becky said loftily. "I can help Mammi take care of him."

"Me, too," Timothy cried.

Caleb swept them both up in a hug. "We'll

all help, ain't so? And we'll all thank God for this day."

Thank You, Lord, Aaron murmured silently. He hadn't done much praying in his recent life, and even those simple words came awkwardly, but he realized he meant them with all his heart.

"We'll put a quart of that vegetable soup in the basket, too," Elizabeth said. She'd started hustling around the kitchen the moment they'd returned and learned of the impending birth. "I wonder…" She glanced in the general direction of the King farm.

"When we take the food over, we'll find out. It's been over two hours since we got back with the midwife."

Sally bent to take the shoofly pies out of the oven. Caleb would be glad of something ready for breakfast tomorrow, and Becky could take a piece in her lunch, as well.

She realized that Elizabeth was watching her, frowning. No doubt she was about to bring up the fact that Sally had gone with Aaron in search of the midwife.

"I wish you hadn't gone alone with him. If you'd just given him the directions…"

"And if he'd failed to find the place?"

Sally closed the oven door a bit more firmly than necessary. "With the baby on the way, I couldn't have done anything else."

"I don't see what all the fuss was about," Ben said. "Sally was just riding in a buggy with him. Any of us would have done the same, with the telephones out and all."

Ben was oblivious of the emotional temperature, as usual, and for once Sally was glad of it. But she suspected that once Elizabeth got him alone, she'd give him an earful.

It was a shame Elizabeth was so busy about Sally's business, but it couldn't hurt her. She could just smile and let it wash over her. Still, she'd be relieved when Mamm and Daad got home.

Elizabeth touched the top of the steak and onion pie she'd made to be sure the dough was done. She turned with a satisfied air. "Everything is ready to pack, I think."

"They'll be sehr glad to see you coming with supper," Ben told her. "Maybe you'll get a look at the new boppli, too."

Elizabeth stiffened. "Sally can take it over," she said quickly.

"But don't you…"

"That's right," Sally said quickly. Ben seemed to have no idea why Elizabeth might find it difficult to go to the King place right now, when they were doubtless rejoicing over a new member of the family.

Sally suppressed an urge to shake him. "I'll be glad to take the basket over." She picked up the basket, and her gaze caught Elizabeth's. They shared an instant of understanding. Then she headed for the door, the loaded basket weighing heavily on her arm.

By the time she'd reached the King place, she'd shifted the basket from one arm to the other several times. She set it down on the porch long enough to rap once and then open the door, carrying the basket to the kitchen.

Here she found Leah in charge and the scent of baking in the air. "I might have known you would beat us here with food," Sally said. "What's the news?"

"It's a boy!" Zeb, clearly elated, grasped her burden and took it to the counter. "A fine, healthy boy, and Jessie is fine, too, thank the gut Lord."

"Ach, that's wonderful gut. I'm sehr happy for all of you."

Zeb nodded. "The Lord does work in mysterious ways, ain't so? There were times I feared Caleb would never be happy again, and now…" He stopped, seeming overcome with emotion.

Sally pressed his arm in understanding. "God has blessed them," she murmured. "Is Caleb up with Jessie?"

"He is." Leah chuckled. "The last time I checked on them, he was sitting there watching them sleep."

"Daniel took the midwife home. Aaron has the young ones helping with chores." Zeb had recovered his usual calm. "And I have been trying to convince Leah that I can handle supper."

"You may as well stop trying. Rebecca and her mamm are taking care of everything there, and you're not getting rid of me until I'm satisfied you're all settled for the night." Leah was firm. "Besides, it smells like Sally has brought most of the supper with her, so it's easily done. Unless you want to push me out the door…"

"Ach, I couldn't do that, now could I?" Zeb took one of the shoofly pies from Sally's basket and sniffed it appreciatively. "You can't lock the doors and windows against kindness—it comes in anyway."

"True enough," Sally said, smiling at the thought. "Is there anything I can do?"

Leah's gaze swept across the various containers on the countertop. "I think we're fine for now with all this food. Denke, Sally. And be sure to thank Elizabeth for us, too."

"I'll be off, then," Sally said. "Ben says he'll be here for the morning milking. Remember to tell Jessie and Caleb we're wonderful happy for them."

She went out, the now-empty basket swinging from her arm. She wasn't, she told herself firmly, upset that she hadn't seen Aaron. That would be silly.

She started down the porch steps just as Aaron came around the large lilac bush at the corner, and her heart gave a glad little leap.

Glancing at her basket, he grinned. "More food. I might have known."

"I think you might," she said, teasing to cover her feelings. "Can you think of an occasion which wouldn't be helped by bringing food?"

"No, I guess I can't. It's kind of you, Sally."

The softness of his glance was turning her to mush inside, and she hurriedly added, "Elizabeth, mostly. I had just started cooking when she and Ben got home, and she swept into action. She's really taken over the kitchen since Mamm and Daad have been away." So much so that sometimes the house felt as if it belonged to her and Ben, instead of being Sally's home.

"Then thank her for us, as well." He was standing very close, and his voice was soft.

"I… I will." She made an effort to control her breath. "So I hear you have a new nephew."

His face lit up. "I never saw such a beautiful baby. Jessie says he looks like Caleb, but I'm not so sure."

"All babies are beautiful, don't you know that?"

"Yes, but it's true about him." He grinned, and Sally's heart seemed to give another shiver of pure joy.

Something was different about Aaron. It was almost, she thought, as if he'd found his place. Her breath caught. If that was true, if he really did think he belonged, then anything might happen. Anything, even for them.

Sally started to walk away, and Aaron realized that he didn't want to let her go. His emotions had been turned upside down today with the worry over Jessie and the baby and the startling conversation he'd had with Caleb. So much had been happening that he hadn't had time to figure it out yet.

But Sally… Sally had somehow seemed to understand his feelings about Caleb even before he did. She'd been the one to point out the thing he'd never taken into account—how young Caleb had been when he'd had to take responsibility for the family.

"Wait."

Sally turned, eyebrows lifted in a question.

"I'll carry your basket for you." He took it from her before she had time to protest. Falling into step, they walked out the lane.

"I could have used you when the basket was filled," she commented.

"Sorry I didn't see you then." He fell silent, not sure how to say what he wanted or even what it was. "You were right," he said finally.

Sally gave him a blank look. "Right?"

"When I was sounding off about Caleb, you said that he'd had to take on a lot of responsibility before he was ready for it." He paused, turning it over in his mind. "I didn't see it at first."

"I know." Her voice was soft, and she seemed to listen intently.

"When our mother left, I was…what? Eight, I guess. I didn't understand what had happened. I just knew that our whole lives had changed in a minute."

"That would be shocking for a child, no matter when or how it happened." Sally's heart was in her eyes. "I imagine a child would feel as if it was his or her fault. And then hide that feeling, for fear of losing the people he had left."

He nodded. Sally's insight astonished him.

"Funny. Now that I think about it, I know I never talked about it to anyone. Daadi didn't tell us anything. It was Caleb who finally told Daniel and me that Mammi had gone away and wasn't coming back."

He heard her sharp, indrawn breath.

"I know." Aaron answered her reaction. "We didn't believe him at first. I remember being so mad I threw my shoe at him. And Daniel ran to the bedroom and hid there."

The memory flooded back…every instant of it. The smell of oatmeal burning on the stove where Caleb had tried to fix it. The cold, hard floor under his stocking feet. The harsh sound of Daniel's sobs. He hadn't consciously thought of it in years, but it was all there, just waiting to spring out and sink its claws into him.

"Surely someone came to help—the neighbors…" Sally's voice died away when he shook his head.

"I guess no one knew at first. Daad just shut himself in the bedroom and locked the door." He drew in a shaky breath. "Caleb did his best to take care of us until Onkel Zeb got here. Onkel Zeb...he made us feel safe. But I still never talked to him about it."

"You couldn't," she said, her voice soft. Gentle. "It probably doesn't help, but that's the way it is with a lot of children when something very bad happens to their family. They can't bring it up because they're afraid that it's their fault, or that if they speak, it will be worse. They need an adult to help them make sense of it."

Aaron gathered his will to push the pain back behind its locked door. When he thought he had it secure, he was able to look at Sally. He studied her face—the warmth in her blue eyes, the caring in her expression.

"An adult like a teacher who cares?"

"Sometimes," she said. "I'd never talk about it, but we often see the results of family trouble in school. At home, everyone's so wrapped up in their own pain they sometimes don't see each other's."

Her words moved through his mind and found acceptance there. Sally had it right. "That's how it was with Daad. He just pulled into himself." He was feeling his way, trying to understand. "Daniel couldn't talk about it... I guess he blamed himself, like you said. And Caleb... Caleb felt he had to take on a man's responsibility when he was just a boy."

It was all becoming so clear to him now. Sally...she was the one who'd helped him see it. If he hadn't come home, he might never have realized the truth. He'd have gone on blaming everyone else for the breakup of their family and shutting himself away from them.

But he had come back, unwilling, forced into it. Maybe that had all been part of God's plan for him.

Sally was patient, giving him time to think it through without questioning. He managed a wry smile, and her troubled face relaxed.

"It's not easy to look at a child's traumatic event like an adult." Her lips curved a little. "You seem to have come a long way."

"No thanks to myself." His voice was rueful. "I had plenty of help. Like you."

Sally shook her head. "I just listened, that's all. You were ready to talk today."

"Yah, and you know why? Because today of all days I got angry with Caleb. I thought he didn't want me to help out. I thought he didn't trust me, didn't want me back. Turned out he was afraid of pushing me into running away again."

They'd reached the end of the lane, and he paused by the fence post. "Strange. I was looking at everything upside down."

"Maybe you were a bit too sensitive," Sally suggested. "Afraid to believe that they wanted you back. Thinking it was too easy."

"Maybe. And maybe you understand people entirely too well to be comfortable." He'd probably regret showing so much of himself to Sally, but not yet.

She studied his face, smiling a little. "Do I make you uncomfortable, Aaron?"

"On the contrary. It's too easy to talk to you. Makes me say things I've never said to a living soul." He tried to say it lightly, but it was true.

She reached out to take her basket, their fingers touching, clinging just for a moment. "You were ready to say them. I just happened to be in the right place, that's all."

"Maybe. Or maybe you were the one person I could say all this to." Gratitude swept through him. "Whichever way it was, thank you, Sally. I'm glad to have all of that out, thanks to you."

Her lips quirked with sudden amusement.

"You make me sound like a medicine. But I'm glad the medicine helped." With a quick lift of her hand, she was gone.

Aaron stood there, watching her walk away from him, thinking how unexpected it all was. He hadn't even thought of Sally when he'd headed for home, but she'd turned out to be the most important part of his homecoming.

Chapter Eight

Sally had to smile at Becky's chatter as they walked home from school on Monday. She was still so excited about her new baby brother that words just bubbled out of her.

"And he woke up in the nighttime, 'cause I heard him crying. Daadi said he was just hungry."

"I'm sure that's true. The boppli's tummy is so small that he needs to eat more often than you do."

Becky nodded, skipping along a little faster. "I wish I got to stay home today like Timothy did. But Mammi said maybe I could help hold the boppli when I got home."

"That will be exciting."

Had Aaron held his little nephew yet? Her mind returned, as it did so frequently, to

Aaron. Bachelors were sometimes reluctant to try, and she'd guess he'd never been around a newborn before.

She ought to put a stop to her tendency to hear his voice in her thoughts...to see his face the way it had looked when he'd confided in her. But she didn't think she could. And besides, what difference did it make? No one, including Aaron, could guess he dominated her thoughts these days.

"They decided on his name, too."

Sally forcibly removed her errant thoughts from Aaron and brought them back to the infant. She tried to focus on Becky's animated face. Each child deserved that kind of attention from her. "So what is it to be? Caleb, after his daadi?"

"Daadi said no. He'll be William, after Mammi's daadi, and Zebulon, after Onkel Zeb." Becky took a few skipping steps. "But we're going to call him Will."

"That sounds like a fine idea. William Zebulon is quite a mouthful for a little baby."

Not Aaron for a name, of course. A brother came farther down on the list of kin to give their name to a new baby.

Frustrated, she realized she was right back to thinking of him. But really, how *could* she fail to muse about what he'd confided yesterday? He'd said things she didn't imagine he'd said to anyone else.

And he'd felt a sense of relief and release when he'd spoken. She'd known it at once, as if she shared his inner thoughts. Hope blossomed within her. Maybe, with his tension and pain about the past eased, Aaron would think seriously about staying.

Becky giggled and hastened her steps as they rounded the bend in the road and could see the farm lanes. Sally's gaze flew to the spot where Aaron had stood waiting for her. But he wasn't there.

Foolish to be disappointed. He was probably busy at home. One small baby could turn things upside down for everyone in the family. He might have to forget about working with Star for a few days.

"Bye, Teacher Sally." Becky ran ahead, pelting down the lane to her family's farmhouse, obviously unable to wait another moment to see her baby brother.

Sally turned down her own lane, lecturing herself about being disappointed over not seeing Aaron. After all, she'd seen a good bit of him the previous day. She couldn't expect to run into him every day, could she?

She was still arguing her way out of disappointment when she spotted Aaron leading Star out of the barn. Her heart gave a leap. She tried to suppress the happiness that danced along her veins at the idea of seeing him. Silly. She was getting as silly as a thirteen-year-old, giggling in the cloakroom because she'd spotted that special boy.

Waving at Aaron, Sally hurried into the house. For once Elizabeth wasn't in the kitchen, so she was able to leave her things on the table and dash out again.

Aaron was leading Star around the buggies again, and as she came up to them, the gelding danced nervously.

"Komm, foolish one," Aaron chided him. "It's just Sally. You know her."

"That's right." She held out her hand with the carrot she'd grabbed from the bin on her way out the door. "You remember treats, anyway."

Velvety lips moved on her palm, and Star began crunching the carrot noisily. While he chomped, she smiled at Aaron.

"How is it with your new nephew today? All well, I hope?"

Aaron's face relaxed in a grin. "Yah, he seems to be ruling the roost at the moment.

Caleb's so delighted he's like a dog with two tails, both wagging. I guess he figured there wouldn't be any more babies after Timothy."

"Until Jessie came along and changed their lives," she finished. "I'm sehr glad. Jessie really longed for a baby, I know."

He raised an eyebrow. "Now, how does a nice young unmarried girl know something like that? I always thought married women were more discreet."

"Some of them are, I suppose." She thought of her sister-in-law, and the attitude that wouldn't let her accept Sally's help. "But Jessie and I have gotten to know each other since she came. She and Leah... Well, they seem to understand that I don't belong with the young single girls any longer."

"You being so very old," he teased.

Before she could find a suitable answer, Star decided to take issue with the wheels of a buggy, trying to back away.

"Enough, you foolish thing." Aaron led him around the buggy again. "Where did Star come from? Was he trained for harness racing?"

"I don't know about his training," she said. "According to my uncle, he was bought off that racetrack out near Scranton."

"He flunked out of racing, in other words." Aaron smiled at her expression. "Don't be offended. Plenty of good buggy horses come from the harness racing world. Star doesn't take to the pacing, though, for all that he looks like a standardbred."

"Would that be why he couldn't make it in harness racing?" She considered Star, liking his smooth, muscular lines and the way he held his head.

"Could be. But it doesn't really matter for a buggy horse. He's got a nice, smooth trot, and he'd do well enough, if we can get him over shying at anything that distracts him."

"That's what you were doing before you came back, then?" she asked tentatively, knowing his time in the Englisch world was a sensitive topic. "Training racing horses?"

He nodded, but he didn't offer anything else, and she didn't feel brave enough to push the subject. If she was patient, maybe one day he'd tell about his life out there. And how it ended.

Aaron gave the horse a pat on the shoulder. "Let's get him harnessed up, and we'll do some more ground driving. He has to get used to the blinders, or he'll be a danger out on the road." He darted a smiling glance at her. "Don't worry. I don't expect to fail."

"Sure of yourself, aren't you?" she said, teasing.

"Only when it comes to horses," he replied.

She saw the truth of it as they worked. Aaron *was* clearly confident about his ability with the horse. She watched as he put the harness on Star, talking constantly as the gelding, at first a little fractious, calmed down in response and stood quietly.

What a gift Aaron had—he was gentle, steady and patient, everything a horse would respond to.

Or a woman, a little voice in her mind observed. Sally tried to ignore it.

Once Star was standing quietly in full harness, Aaron nodded to Sally to pick up the lines. "I'll walk at his head for a bit while you drive him. You're the boss, and he has to get used to your voice."

She adjusted the lines in her hands, telling herself she wasn't at all nervous, and more than a little aware of Aaron's gaze on her. "Now, Star." She collected the gelding's attention. "Walk on." She accompanied the words with a small movement of her hands.

To her pleasure—and a little surprise—Star

walked on quietly. Obviously Aaron's slow and steady training was paying off. Each of her own attempts to drive Star had been a battle from the start.

They walked the horse around and around the barnyard. Understanding what Aaron wanted, she steered Star close to the various obstacles that might be expected to distract him. There wasn't the faintest hesitation as he moved along.

"Gut boy," she said, unable to keep the exhilaration out of her voice. She flashed Aaron a smile. "You really are a wonder worker, ain't so?"

"It's all a matter of patience. And listening to the animal. It tells you what it wants and what it's afraid of if you only listen."

"Well, you clearly heard what Star was saying better than I did."

"Maybe I'm more used to listening." He looked at her, a challenge in his eyes. "Are you ready for me to step away from his head?"

A little flutter teased her stomach as she took the challenge. "For sure. Let's see how he does without you."

Predictably, Star turned his head to watch as Aaron moved away. But when Sally clucked to him, he moved on obediently.

She grinned, picking up the speed a little so that he broke into a slow trot. Sally jogged along behind him, her attention all on the horse. She was doing it. This was going to work out, and she'd have the freedom that her own buggy horse gave her. Exhilaration carried her along.

"Watch out—"

Aaron's warning came an instant too late. She stepped into a depression in the ground and lost her balance, coming down heavily. Even as she saw the ground rushing at her, she held onto the lines and managed to halt Star even as she sprawled in the grass.

Star stopped, standing quietly even though he must have been aware that something was wrong behind him. Sally was so pleased that she hardly noticed her sprawled position until Aaron reached her. He knelt next to her, reaching out to clasp her shoulders.

"Sally, are you hurt? Can you move?" The concern in his voice warmed her.

"I'm fine, I think." She moved her legs and found that everything worked. "Nothing hurt but my dignity."

She could feel his tension relax. "You held on to the lines. That's the most important thing."

"Ach, no. The most important thing is that Star is standing quietly, thanks to you."

She looked up into his face as she spoke, startled to find him so close. It felt as if she could feel the warmth radiating from his skin, and she took in the fresh, masculine scent of him.

Awareness flooded her. She tried to look away, but it was impossible. All she could do was sit there in the grass with Aaron's hands strong on her shoulders and his lips inches from hers.

He sucked in a breath, and his eyes darkened. He drew even closer, until she could imagine his lips on hers, gentle and demanding at the same time.

And then, too quickly, he pulled back, leaving her with her lips parted and her skin chilled by the sudden loss of his warmth.

"If you're sure you aren't hurt, let me help you up." His hands moved to her elbows. His tone was cool, his face impassive, and her heart winced in pain.

"I can manage…" she began, but he had already lifted her to her feet and taken a step away.

A flurry of movement at the edge of her vision warned her. Elizabeth came running toward them. Aaron must have seen her before Sally did. Relief swept through her.

"Sally, what happened? That horse—"

"No, we can't blame Star. I wasn't watching where I was going, and I stepped in a hole." She looked down, scuffing at the hole with the toe of her shoe. "Next thing I knew I was sitting on the ground, but Star stood perfectly the whole time." She couldn't help the note of triumph in her voice.

"Yah, well, that's a gut thing." It was a grumbling concession, but probably the best Elizabeth could do. She put her arm around Sally's waist. "Komm in the house and let me make sure you're not hurt. You could have twisted an ankle, falling like that. Aaron will take care of the horse, ain't so?"

"Of course." Aaron's tone was carefully polite.

"But we weren't finished—" she protested, but now Aaron interrupted her.

"Just about. I'll walk him around a few more minutes, and then unharness him. Next time we'll hitch him to the buggy."

"Are you sure Star is ready for that?" Maybe Star was, but she had to confess that she wasn't ready for the training to end.

"Aaron is the trainer," Elizabeth said. "I'm

sure he knows best. Besides, he'll be wanting to finish up so he'll be free to…do whatever he plans to do next."

They all knew what she meant by that, didn't they? Elizabeth was pushing Aaron for a decision. Was he staying or going? The fact that Sally longed to know the answer didn't make it any easier to forgive Elizabeth for pressing.

"Go along and relax," Aaron said, his voice colorless, his face turned away. "We'll work again tomorrow."

He took Star and began walking him around, leaving her with nothing to say, even if she could have come up with something.

Aaron knew perfectly well what Elizabeth had been doing. She'd seen them close together and come running out to save her sister-in-law from him. Or maybe from herself. He understood, all right.

He swung his leg and kicked a chunk of gravel from the lane, sending it soaring toward a fence post. Unfortunately it missed. He'd have preferred a satisfying plop.

Still, he supposed it was just as well that Elizabeth hadn't been near enough to see their expressions. Then she'd really have panicked. He'd been close to it himself.

Where was the guilt he should feel? Instead of regretting it, all Aaron could do was picture Sally's face so close to his, with her blue eyes filled with longing, her lips…

Now the guilt did wash over him. He'd lived in the outside world too long if he could feel that way for Sally. What Sally felt was an extension of the hero worship she'd had for him as a child, and that couldn't be a solid basis for anything. In some ways, despite her maturity and her surprising wisdom, she was still that little girl.

Well, maybe not a little girl. Sally had improved with age, but as for him—he seemed to see himself reflected in the clear blue of her eyes. She still saw her hero, but he saw the truth. He was older, worn away by everything that had happened to him. He was no longer capable of being the person Sally needed and deserved. And there was the central, impossible barrier between them—he wasn't Amish any longer.

By the time Aaron reached the farmhouse he was in no mood to inflict himself on the rest of the family. He headed for the barn. There was always something to do there, preferably something that pushed his muscles to their utmost and dulled his mind.

A solid hour of mucking out stalls brought with it a measure of calm. The repetitive movements, the play of muscles against his shirt, the familiar sounds and smells of a stable…they all had the ability to soothe the senses, at least for him. He could even smile at the thought of recommending such therapy for some of the people he'd known.

At least now he was in the proper mood to go inside and inflict himself on other people.

He'd stopped outside the house to scrape the dirt from his shoes when he saw a buggy coming down the farm lane toward him. Automatically he stepped forward to take the horse's head as it reached him.

The driver nodded his thanks, and Aaron's momentary peace vanished at the sight of the bishop. In the next instant Bishop Thomas had turned back to lift down a basket, and Aaron could breathe again. Bishop Thomas had obviously come because of Jessie and the new baby, not him.

"I'll take care of the horse and buggy, Bishop Thomas. You go right on in."

"Denke, Aaron. But you were on your way inside, as well, ain't so?"

It seemed he wouldn't be allowed to slip away out of sight. "As soon as I finish cleaning up." He managed to smile. "Leah's in charge, and she'll kick me out if I bring the stable smell into her clean kitchen."

Aaron delayed it as long as he could. Bishop Thomas was a fine person, but he wasn't ready for any questions about his faith or his intentions. But finally he had to go inside.

He found everyone gathered around Caleb, who held his tiny son while the others clustered around him. Timothy was on the edge, standing on tiptoe trying to see his baby brother, so Aaron picked him up from behind and hoisted, making the boy giggle.

"Is that better? What do you think? Does he look like you?"

Timothy's forehead crinkled as he tried to imagine his image in that tiny face. "I think he just looks like a boppli."

The adults chuckled, but Becky shook her head. "I remember you when you were little, and you looked a lot like Will."

"I wasn't ever that little," he declared.

Caleb grinned and reached out to tickle him. "Yah, you were. But you grew fast."

"Babies have a way of doing that," Bishop Thomas said, his voice gentle. He reached out to touch the baby's head lightly. "The gut Lord be with you, William."

They were all silent for a moment. Then the bishop stepped back, smiling. "Now I must go, or I'll be late for supper and my wife won't like that. Will you walk out with me, Aaron?"

Caught. Aaron obviously didn't have a choice. He held the door and followed Bishop Thomas outside, bracing himself for whatever words of wisdom the bishop wanted to impart.

Nothing was said as they moved to the horse and buggy together. There Bishop Thomas paused, turning to put a strong hand on Aaron's shoulder. "So, Aaron. How are you doing, now that you have been home for a time?"

Aaron didn't want to meet his eyes, but he couldn't help doing so. At least he didn't read any condemnation there. "All right. But I haven't made any decisions about the future, if that's what you're asking."

It occurred to him that wasn't the best of responses, but Bishop Thomas didn't seem offended. Instead, he just looked curious. "What is it that holds you back, do you think?"

Aaron shrugged, feeling inarticulate. How did he put it into words? "I don't know. It's just…when I think about kneeling in front of everyone, confessing I've done wrong…"

"Ach, Aaron, do you think you're the first to stumble? We have heard worse." He had a rueful smile. "Anyway, that's looking too far ahead."

Aaron could only stare at the bishop blankly. "Too far ahead? That's surely the first step, isn't it?"

"Ach, no." The bishop paused, as if trying to think how to explain something to a child, and Aaron waited, tense, torn between wanting to hear and wanting to run away.

"If God is calling you back," Bishop Thomas said slowly, "His voice will get so strong that there will be no doubting it. And when that time comes, nothing else will matter the least little bit. You see?"

Aaron shook his head. He didn't see, and he couldn't imagine it.

Bishop Thomas chuckled. "You are like Timothy, unable to see that he'd ever been that small. Just wait, and listen for God's voice. It will come, in His time. And in the meantime, will you commit to living by the Ordnung for a time...say, for a month?"

He was torn, not wanting to commit to anything unless he could be sure. But the bishop was waiting. Finally, reluctantly, he nodded.

"I'll try. For one month."

"Gut." Bishop Thomas clapped him on the shoulder. "Now stop worrying about it. Just listen. God will make it clear."

Aaron wasn't sure whether he hoped the bishop was right or wrong.

Chapter Nine

When Sally had reached the house, she'd made a quick excuse to scurry up to her room, eager to avoid the lecture Elizabeth seemed primed to deliver. She'd said she had to change her muddied dress and do some schoolwork, which was true enough.

But instead of doing so, fifteen minutes later she found herself standing with a clean dress in her hands, completely lost in her thoughts, while Aaron's face filled her mind.

Those moments when they'd looked into each other's eyes—she couldn't be mistaken about what she felt, not now. Dropping the dress, she sank down onto the bed, pressing her palms to her hot cheeks. She loved him. She was in love with Aaron King.

For years she'd convinced herself that she

could never risk making a mistake again, but now she knew how foolish she'd been to think she could lock love out of her life.

She hadn't known enough about love. She hadn't realized that love, real love, was like the rush of a mighty river...a strong, deep current that swept away every doubt. No matter what she did or didn't do about it, she loved Aaron.

That love swept away every doubt for her, but what about for Aaron? What she felt didn't matter in the least if Aaron didn't feel the same.

For a moment when they'd touched, when their unguarded gazes had crossed, she'd been sure of what she saw in his eyes. She'd been convinced he loved her, and her heart had sung with the sheer joy of it.

But the moment had passed. He'd backed away first. She couldn't deny that or rationalize it. Aaron had retreated. She'd told herself that he'd stopped because he'd spotted Elizabeth watching them.

But what if she'd been wrong? What if he'd seen the love shining in her eyes and withdrew, embarrassed at the thought that little Sally was in love with him?

The blood seemed to pound in her head,

and for an instant her face burned while her hands turned icy cold. Humiliation swept over her, and all her hope seemed to shrivel away to nothing. If Aaron had seen that she loved him and he didn't return her feelings, how could she ever face him again?

Maybe she should be glad that Elizabeth had interrupted them when she did. Maybe that interruption had saved her from still worse embarrassment...the agony of seeing Aaron try to find a way to let her down easy.

Gathering the threads of her confidence together, Sally straightened, her palms pressing into the quilt beneath her. The truth was that she didn't know.

And she didn't have any choice. She and Aaron couldn't avoid each other. They were neighbors, united in so many ways. That meant she'd have to hang on to her self-control regardless of what Aaron might feel.

What would he do? If it had been real, if he'd seen her feelings and returned them, he would speak to her. Naturally he would. And if he didn't? For a moment her mind was blank. She didn't have any illusions that Aaron hadn't seen her feelings—she knew how quick and intuitive he was.

He'd try to spare her. He'd carry on just as

usual, as if nothing had happened. He'd want her to be able to save face.

She'd require a lot more control than she'd shown so far if that were to happen. She'd best start practicing. So right now she'd get dressed, go downstairs and hope Elizabeth had been distracted from the lecture she'd been so eager to give.

With a silent prayer for guidance, Sally pulled the dress over her head and smoothed her hair back. She'd make herself presentable, and she'd move forward. She didn't have the luxury of sitting here feeling sorry for herself.

Slipping into the kitchen, Sally found Elizabeth standing at the stove, her back turned. When she didn't immediately spin around and start talking, Sally breathed a sigh of relief. Maybe the worst was over.

With a glance at the clock, Sally pulled plates from the cabinet and began setting the table. Usually this was such a pleasant part of the day—when life was normal, that was. She and Mamm would chatter away about everything and nothing while they got supper on.

Mamm always loved to hear her stories of what had happened at school with the children that day, and Sally knew she could say anything and name names without fear that folks would get to hear about it.

She couldn't do that with Elizabeth. First because Elizabeth didn't really seem interested in her tales of her scholars. And second, because she didn't feel absolutely confident that something she said might not be repeated. Elizabeth wouldn't do that deliberately, but she liked to talk, and she didn't always stop to think about what was coming out when she did.

The continued silence from Elizabeth began to feel a little ominous. It wasn't like her to hold her fire for this long. She must be really perturbed about what she probably saw as Sally's misbehavior.

Finally Sally moved over next to her. "What can I do?"

"Nothing for supper." Elizabeth shot her a glance. "But you can listen to me instead of running off."

So that was it. There was no point in pretending she hadn't done what she clearly had.

"I'm sorry, Elizabeth. But I didn't want to get into an argument about Aaron." She had to force her voice to remain level when she said his name.

"It's not Aaron I'm worried about." Elizabeth slapped the wooden spoon she was holding down on the counter. "It's you. I looked out the window and what did I see? I saw you down on the ground with Aaron's arms around you."

Sally held on to her tongue with an effort. "I already explained what happened. I stepped in a hole and tripped. Naturally Aaron came to see if I was hurt, just like you did."

"And what about him having his arms around you, and you looking up at him?"

"He was trying to help me up. And I was laughing at my own clumsiness, that was all." That wasn't all, of course, but she couldn't tell Elizabeth the rest of it. How everything she thought she knew about herself was changed in that instant their eyes met—no, she couldn't tell Elizabeth that.

"What if someone else had seen you?" Elizabeth wasn't accepting it. "What if the bishop had been passing by and had seen you and Aaron with his arms around you? Aaron's just an Englischer now, for all that you were friends when you were a child. You can't get involved with him."

"I'm not involved. I'm just being a friend. And if Aaron wants to repent and come back to the Leit, I won't do anything to make that harder for him." Tears stung her eyes, but she wouldn't let them spill over. "What if everyone acted that way? He'd never want to stay then."

Elizabeth's broad cheeks flushed. "I'm not saying we should be mean to him. I'm saying that you're an unmarried woman and a teacher besides, and you need to mind your reputation. What would your mamm and daad say if they were here?"

"They wouldn't scold me for being kind to an old friend." Her voice was probably a little too tart. "And they'd give me credit for being grown-up enough to make my own decisions."

"Your decisions?" Elizabeth took fire in an instant. "Like throwing over a gut man who wanted to marry you? And taking up with someone who's a runaway and a rebel and thinks and acts like an Englischer? You should be ashamed to cause folks to talk about you."

"You're the only one who's talking about me," she snapped, her control breaking. "You have no business telling me what to do. I'm not your child."

In the instant she said the words Sally wanted them back. But that couldn't be done. Her unruly tongue had led her into hurting Elizabeth. No matter what the provocation was, she ought to know better if she was as grown-up as she'd declared herself to be.

"I'm sorry." She rushed into speech. "Elizabeth, I didn't mean to say that. I'm so sorry."

Elizabeth clamped her lips closed, shaking her head. She turned back to the stove, but not before Sally saw the tears spill over on her cheeks.

The autumn air smelled fresh and clear the next morning after a brief rain overnight, and the yellows and oranges of the trees on the ridge seemed to shine. Aaron bent to disconnect the battery that ran the electric fence around the west pasture. As often happened, the wire had become grounded somewhere, so he meant to find it before any of the cows decided to go roaming. Usually some wise old cow could find a spot and lean on it until she'd broken through to some grass she thought greener.

"There'll be a small branch down on it somewhere after the rain." Onkel Zeb walked alongside him as they started checking the fence line.

"Most likely." Aaron darted a glance at his uncle. So far no one had asked him what the bishop had said to him, and he'd been grateful. Was Onkel Zeb giving him a chance to talk?

Not that he wasn't willing to tell his uncle, but since yesterday he'd been too preoccupied with his thoughts about Sally to concentrate on anything else. Those moments when they'd been so close to each other… Looking into her eyes had been like sinking into a deep blue pool, leaving him warm and weightless and safe.

Reality had burst in soon enough. Elizabeth had plainly been horrified at the thought of him with her young sister-in-law. Most likely anyone else from the community who saw them would feel the same.

Face it, they would all know he was too old for Sally, both in years and in experience. His time out in the world had changed him.

And yet Sally didn't seem to mind that. She just reached right past the forbidding surface changes and touched his heart. Maybe he could deny what he felt to anyone else, but it was stupid to deny it to himself. He was more than halfway in love with her already.

He came out of his abstraction to see Onkel Zeb kneeling to pull some weeds away from the wire.

"Here, I'll get that." He knelt quickly, annoyed with himself for not doing his job.

"I'm not ready for the rocking chair yet," Zeb said, his tone mild, but he sat back on his heels and made room for Aaron to pull the weeds. But even as he spoke, he reached out to grab the fence post to pull himself up to standing. "Though I won't say a helping hand isn't wilkom now and then."

Aaron grinned at him. "Are you trying to make me feel useful?"

"I don't need to try. It's a fact," Zeb said bluntly. "With Daniel as busy as he is with his carpentry business and the young ones too little to be much help, we need another man around here." He paused as if to let that sink in.

"I'm not sure..." Aaron began, thinking he wasn't that man.

Onkel Zeb swept on. "There's plenty of folks around who'd be interested in a good horse trainer, too, with horses getting so popular among the Englisch. You put up a couple of signs in some stores, and you'd get all the business you can handle."

He didn't know if that was true, but he appreciated Onkel Zeb's effort to make him feel there was a place for him here. "Have you been talking to the bishop, by chance?"

Zeb shook his head. "No, why? Is that what he told you?"

"Not exactly." He hesitated, but he guessed it might as well come out. "He asked me to agree to live by the Ordnung for a month before I made a decision about the future."

The future...and Sally's face forming in his mind, smiling at him.

"Bishop Tom is a wise man. You're taking his advice, ain't so?"

"I guess I am. But I don't know how it will turn out." Aaron hurried to add that, afraid his uncle would read too much into his cooperation. He wasn't even sure if he could do it in the long run.

But if he could, it was so tempting to think he could have a future here.

Onkel Zeb straightened, shielding his eyes as he glanced toward the lane. "There's Ben Stoltzfus coming over." He waved, catching Ben's eye, and Ben left the lane and crossed the field toward them.

"I guess he's looking for us." Aaron stood waiting. And wondering. Was it a coincidence that Ben showed up apparently wanting to talk the day after his Elizabeth had seen Aaron and Sally touching? He didn't think so.

Ben reached them. "Zeb. Aaron. A fine day, ain't so?"

"It is that," Zeb replied. "Are you needing something, Ben?"

Ben looked from Aaron to Zeb and back again, and embarrassment made his already ruddy face a bright red. "Chust a word or two with Aaron, if he can spare the time."

Aaron stiffened. So it was like he'd figured. "I need to walk round the fence line. Come along, if you want."

There was an awkward silence. Finally Zeb seemed to get the idea. "If you've got Ben helping you, I guess you don't need me, yah? I'll go see if there's coffee hot on the stove."

"That's fine. Save some coffee for me."

Waiting until he was sure Onkel Zeb was out of earshot, Aaron pulled a leafy twig off the wire. When he looked up Ben was still standing there, looking like a man who'd rather be anywhere else. Some of Aaron's irritation ebbed.

"Let me guess. Elizabeth wants you to talk to me about Sally."

Ben stared at him for a moment, and then a self-conscious grin spread across his face.

"You know women. If they don't have something to worry about, they invent something. I'm that sorry about this."

Aaron shrugged. "No need to worry. I understand. Elizabeth saw me helping Sally up when she fell. Sounds as if she got the wrong idea."

"That's it." Ben sounded relieved. "Sally told her there was nothing to it, but Elizabeth gets nervous. She feels like we're responsible for Sally while the folks are away."

So Sally said there was nothing to it, did she? He was taken aback for a moment. He knew what he'd felt. Surely he didn't imagine what he'd seen in Sally's face. But he ought to be relieved if she didn't make anything of it.

"There's no need to worry about Sally, not where I'm concerned." He walked a few more feet along the fence and pulled out the small branch that had gotten entangled with the wire with one end touching the ground. That was probably the source of the trouble. It didn't take much to cause a problem, did it?

"Well, that's what I thought. I mean, Sally's just a kid."

Aaron looked at him, his eyebrows lifting. "I don't think your little sister is a kid anymore. She's been kind to me since I got back, and I appreciate it."

"Yah, well, Sally has a kind heart." Ben scuffed at a clod of dirt. "I guess it is hard for you, coming back to all this quiet after the life you've had out there."

What kind of life was Ben imagining? Probably nothing close to the truth.

"It wasn't all that different. Taking care of the horses, mucking out stalls…nothing exciting about that."

Ben didn't respond. He'd always been kind of slow of speech, but right now he looked like he was at a complete loss. Aaron sighed. He couldn't expect Ben to understand. All he could do was reassure him.

"Look, the fact is I'm not going to court Sally or anyone else unless and until I make up my mind to stay. So tell Elizabeth she can stop worrying."

The words had come out with an edge, but he couldn't help that. Okay, so Ben was embarrassed, but he'd started it. He couldn't expect Aaron to like having someone else tell him what he ought to do or feel.

Since Ben still seemed bereft of words, Aaron turned away. "If that's all, I need to finish with the fence and get the battery back on again."

"Yah, um, denke." Ben was back to shuffling his feet again. "Denke."

Aaron didn't bother watching him walk away. He was too busy trying to get himself back under control. Okay, it wasn't entirely Ben's fault. He understood that Elizabeth had done most of the pushing. But that didn't mean he had to like having other people interfering in his life. In contrast with this, the total disinterest of most of the people he'd met in the Englisch world looked pretty good to him right now.

As soon as Sally got home, she saw that Aaron had Star hitched up to the buggy already. He hadn't waited for her.

Sally rushed into the house, dropped her books and hurried back out again. But no sooner had she stepped off the porch than her brother appeared, holding out a hand to stop her. "Can we talk for a minute?"

Impatient, she shook her head. "I'm late to work with Star. We'll talk later."

Ben clasped her sleeve. "Wait. I... I have to tell you something."

She read her brother with an experienced

glance. Ben was embarrassed, and judging by the way he was hanging his head, he'd done something he wished he hadn't. Something to do with her, clearly.

"Okay. What did you do?"

His eyes flickered toward her and then away. "You're going to be mad, but… I talked to Aaron about you." He held up his hand before she could speak. "I know, I know. You're mad. I guess I shouldn't have, but Elizabeth was so worried—" He stopped abruptly, as if he hadn't intended to say that.

Elizabeth was worried. Elizabeth was also far too fond of interfering in other people's business. But given the hurtful thing she'd said to Elizabeth, she was just as guilty.

She said a quick prayer for calm. "There's no reason for either of you to be worried. I'm all grown-up now, Ben. I know it's hard to believe, but I don't need you or Elizabeth to protect me."

"Yah, yah, but it's not so easy for me." He tried the effect of a smile, but she didn't really feel like smiling back. "You've been my little sister for a long time."

"That doesn't mean you ought to embarrass me that way. Or Aaron. What must he have thought?"

Ben actually looked a little relieved by her scolding words. "Aaron's okay. He didn't get mad. He just said there wasn't anything going on. Said he wasn't courting anybody—he doesn't even know yet if he's staying. So you see, it's all right."

It wasn't all right, but she couldn't see any point to telling Ben so. He'd meant well, she supposed.

"Yah, okay," she murmured, turning away.

But it wasn't all right. Her cheeks were flushed, and her heart was pummeled by a whole mix of emotions—embarrassment, humiliation and disappointment. No, *disappointment* wasn't a strong enough word. All her hope had been dashed to pieces by a few words.

So there was nothing going on between them, was there? She knew what she'd seen in his face, but that didn't matter, not if he chose to ignore it. So it was over before it began, and now she had to face Aaron and pretend she wasn't hurt.

Sally was dreading finding the words to say to Aaron, but he saved her the trouble, pulling Star to a halt and hurrying into speech.

"Star's behaving himself with the buggy.

He doesn't seem to object to the harness and blinders at all. You come up and give it a try."

Aaron held out his hand to help her up, but Sally grabbed the edge of the seat and swung herself up easily. So they were going to pretend nothing had happened, were they? In that case, it might be best if they didn't touch.

He handed her the lines. "Just take him up by the barn and circle round. Let's see how he does."

Nodding, Sally clucked to Star and they started smoothly off toward the barn. Star was responding beautifully, but it was hard to concentrate when her mind was filled with so many more important things.

They made a couple of circles before going out the lane, turning and coming back in again. And the whole time Aaron didn't say a word.

Finally he spoke. "Star's turned out to be a quick learner once we got over a few bumps." Aaron was staring straight ahead, over the horse's ears. "Go back out the lane again, and we'll see how he does on the road."

She nodded, circling smoothly before going out the lane. She sent a quick sideways glance toward Aaron. "You don't have to be so careful around me. Ben told me what he said to you. He's downright embarrassed, and it serves him right. I'm so sorry."

"No reason for you to be sorry. Ben's your big brother. He's never going to stop thinking of you as his little sister who needs protecting." The words were spoken casually, but he didn't look at her.

Anger flared, but she controlled it. She was getting tired of everyone referring to her as little. It was bad enough for Ben. Or did Aaron mean that *he* could never see her as anything but Ben's little sister?

Aaron didn't seem to think anything else needed to be said, but she couldn't quite let it go.

"You may be right about Ben, but I'm not Elizabeth's little sister, and I know perfectly well this came from her."

"Turn down toward the school," he said, nodding when Star moved obediently past the spot where he'd thrown a fit that day Aaron arrived.

He waited until they covered a few yards along the road before he spoke again. "Ben says Elizabeth feels responsible because your parents are away."

"In that case, I wish they'd hurry up and come back." Hurt made her voice sharp.

Aaron really was acting as if those moments between them had never been.

He chuckled, a low bass note that seemed to set up an answering echo in her.

"All right. I know that sounds childish," she admitted. "I do try when it comes to Elizabeth."

"From what I've seen, it would take a lifetime of patience."

"Something I don't have, I guess. She means well, and she does care about me." She could actually smile with him over Elizabeth's quirks. "Shall I pull in to the school?"

"Yah, let's see what Star thinks of the school grounds."

By the time they'd reached the school, she was congratulating herself on her control. Aaron was behaving normally with her, as if those moments between them had never happened.

So that meant she had to do the same. No one needed to know what she felt about a dream that wasn't going to come true.

And then Aaron's hand brushed hers as he gestured for her to turn, and the warmth of that touch swept along her skin and straight to her heart, and she wanted to cry.

Chapter Ten

Afraid her emotions were going to overwhelm her, Sally pulled up in front of the small porch of the school. "Since we're here, I need to pick up something." She muttered the words, shoved the lines into Aaron's hands and jumped down.

Thank the gut Lord, Aaron didn't question her about the sudden decision. As she hurried inside, she heard him click to Star, and then came the sound of the horse and buggy moving around the schoolhouse.

Sally didn't stop until she reached her desk. Then she stood there, hands planted on the flat surface for support, and fought back the tears that threatened to overflow. A few tears trickled onto her cheeks, and she wiped them away with the back of her hand.

This was so foolish. She'd run out on a reasonable chance of marriage only to fall hard for the one man who wasn't interested. She'd been wrong to think he felt anything. He couldn't possibly be so casual if he did.

Some would say that it served her right to be hurt in the same way she'd hurt Fred. And if she went around moping and showing her feelings this way, soon half the church would guess what had happened between them.

That realization brought her upright in a hurry. Whatever happened, she would not give away her feelings—not to Aaron or anyone else.

Alerted by the thud of footsteps on the wooden porch, Sally managed to be rummaging through a file drawer by the time Aaron came in. He wandered up through the rows of desks, touching one here and there, as if remembering the past.

"Find what you wanted?"

She pulled out a file folder at random. "Yah, this is it. I'm glad we came back this way, or I'd have missed it too late to come back for it."

"Good. Just tell me one thing. Why are there two harrows and a baby crib behind the shed?"

"Oh, no." Annoyance chased away the last

of her mood. "I've told people so many times not to leave things here for the auction until the day before. It's just plain dangerous having such things out where the scholars play during recess."

"I don't suppose you want them to play out by the shed, but I get your meaning. Anything like that would have been an irresistible lure when I was a kid."

"Of course. They'd be trying to hitch each other up to the harrow before I knew it." She shoved the drawer closed with a bang. "The auction's not until Saturday. I appreciate having folks bring things for the school auction, but—"

"But you wish they'd follow directions." He smiled. "Shall I go out and drag them into the shed?"

"That's all right. Don't bother. I'll have some of the older boys do it first thing in the morning. What were you doing out back?"

He perched on the corner of her desk. "Showing Star his accommodations for when you drive him to school. He seems to approve of the stall and the paddock. Acts like he's right at home."

"That's wonderful good news. I was afraid I'd never be able to drive him to school." *See?*

she told herself. *You can carry on a perfectly normal conversation with him and not feel so much as a twinge.*

"He's a perfect gentleman. Good, since this is his final lesson."

The words fell on Sally like a blow. "F-final?" She stammered the word. "You're leaving? Going back to your job?"

"No." His face tightened for an instant. "I just meant Star has learned enough to go on with. I don't expect you to have any trouble with him. He deserves a gold star. Or at least a happy face sticker."

Sally managed a smile. How could she be so stupid? She'd best not congratulate herself on her control too soon.

"I think I have some. But he'd probably prefer a bite of apple."

"Most likely." Aaron rose, moving to the chalkboard and back seemingly at random. "Onkel Zeb thinks I can pick up a few more horses to train once word gets around. I'd like that."

He seemed distracted, frowning and tense. Had she said something, done something to bring this on?

Then he swung around to look at her with an air of decision. "You mentioned my job.

But I can't go back to it. If I did, I'd probably end up in jail."

Sally, wordless, stared at him, her thoughts tumbling wildly out of control.

"Well?" His face gave a wry twist, maybe to cover pain. "Aren't you going to run away from me?"

She found her voice. "I don't run away from my friends."

"Why not? It's what any respectable Amish maidal would do, isn't it?"

He couldn't hide the pain, not from her. She read it in the darkness of his eyes, the set of his mouth and the tension that radiated from him so strongly it nearly knocked her back a step.

"I've never worried too much about whether folks thought I was respectable or not." She hesitated, knowing she had to say more. Afraid of giving away too much. But Aaron's obvious pain was more important than her feelings.

"Whatever happened, I know one thing for sure. I know that you didn't do anything wrong."

Aaron was stunned into silence. Whatever response he'd expected, it certainly hadn't been that simple, honest statement of faith in him.

"Denke," he murmured.

She nodded. And just stood there, waiting. Not asking anything, not offering advice. Just waiting in case he wanted to tell her more.

To his amazement, for the first time since it had happened, he wanted to speak. He wanted to tell Sally all of it.

He ran a hand through his hair. Where to begin? How could Sally, with no experience of that world, possibly understand?

"Out in Indiana I got a job with a man who ran a racing stable. Harness racing, you know?"

She nodded.

"Albert Winfield, his name is. I was fortunate. I went looking for work without knowing anything about the people, and I ended up with one of the best owners in the business." He paused, thinking of the impression Mr. Winfield had made on him. "A good horseman, but more than that. A good man. Honest, respected."

"The right person for you to work for," she said softly, encouraging him to go on.

"He was in the stables and the training grounds every day. I guess he watched me, and he decided I could do more than shovel stalls." He remembered so clearly the day Winfield had found him working a horse for one of the trainers who was hungover. "Pretty soon I was working as a trainer."

"That made you happy, ain't so?" Again that soft voice, and he realized she was talking to him the way he talked to the horses. And it was having a similar effect. He felt his tension easing and his breath slowing.

"Yah. He had faith in me. After a season he promoted me to head trainer. His horses did well, and he gave me the credit." He shrugged, thinking of the man's generosity. "A lot of the success was in the good, honest stock he brought in. Anyway, we worked together, and I was..." He hesitated, not sure what was the right word.

"Happy?" she suggested.

"Yah, that, but I started to feel like maybe one day I could belong." He let his eyes meet hers. "You don't understand how lost you can be out in the Englisch world. It feels like there's no place you really fit in. Anyway, Winfield did that for me."

He sucked in a breath, feeling the tension returning. How could he say the rest of it to Sally, of all people?

"And then things started to go wrong." Again she didn't ask. She just said the words that made it easier to speak.

"I met a woman—she was involved in the racing circuit. She started showing up to watch me working the young horses. Pretty soon we were seeing each other." He carefully didn't look at Sally. "One night we'd gone out to supper and ran into someone she knew. She introduced me, and next thing I knew we were sitting with him. He was another owner."

"Quite a coincidence," she murmured.

"Yah." He managed a rueful smile. "I was stupid. Flattered that she wanted to see me, that I was sitting there talking to one of the big men in the business. And he made me an offer. Seemed like he knew just what I made, and he topped it. Said we could do great things together—I could help him pick out the best new stock, train them, have things all my way."

He shot a glance at Sally, but she didn't speak.

"So I thought about it. But I liked where I was—liked working with a man I respected. Winfield—he thought more about the horses than the glory of winning. So I said no, I wanted to stay where I was. I figured that was the end of it."

His jaw tightened so much that he could hardly speak. But he had to tell the rest of it. The pressure rose in him to get it out. Sally was safe. He could say anything to her.

"I didn't say anything to Winfield about the offer. I didn't want him to think I was angling for a raise. But I should have. In the next day's race, one of our horses turned out to be drugged."

Sally didn't say anything, but he heard her sharp indrawn breath.

"Someone had told Winfield about seeing me with the other owner. Winfield...he had a quick temper. He blew up, accused me, didn't give me a chance to defend myself."

He was back in that office again, with Winfield standing behind the big desk. The walls were covered with photographs...some of them horses he'd trained, and there was a shelf full of trophies. The whole place was a tribute to Winfield Stables...to the sterling reputation Winfield had always had in the business. A reputation he thought Aaron had ruined.

He forced himself to go on. "Winfield said he'd bring the police in. I guess I lost it then. I wouldn't even try to explain to someone who judged me like that. I stamped out, packed my gear and left. Everything was gone, and all I wanted was to get lost."

The bitterness was still an acrid taste in his mouth, wounding his soul.

"So you came home."

"Yah. I came home."

He'd spilled it all. It had made him angry and hurt and ashamed all over again, but oddly enough it was a relief…like lancing a boil and letting all the poison out.

Gratitude swept over him. Sally wasn't the little tagalong of his youth or the desirable woman she'd become. She was a source of the belief and comfort he needed more than anything else in the world right now.

He didn't begin to know what to say to her. How to thank her. He looked at her, to find her frowning a little, a question in her eyes after all that time of listening.

"But, Aaron, didn't you ever tell Mr. Winfield the truth about what happened?"

"He didn't want to hear it." Remembered anger moved in him. "I wasn't going to beg for a chance to explain. He should have known me better than to think I'd do such a thing. Why should I try to explain?"

"I see." She studied his face and then

glanced away, as if not liking what she saw there. "You know, your Mr. Winfield sort of reminds me of someone I know. Someone who has a quick temper and flares up and says things he doesn't mean…things he's sorry for later but can't swallow his pride and say so."

Sally knew him too well. She was talking about him, and much as he'd like to deny it, what she said was true.

Well, true or not, the thing was over and done with. "I can't do anything about it now."

She shrugged. "Maybe not. But maybe he's had second thoughts. Maybe after he cooled off, he wanted to hear what you had to say but couldn't, because you'd gone. And he doesn't know how to find you."

"Forget it. I don't need that job any longer." He tried to sound convincing. But somehow he knew that Sally's words had planted a seed. What he did about it was up to him.

Sally studied his face, her heart breaking for him. She longed to reach out, to touch him in comfort, but somehow she knew she had to let him make the first move toward her.

He shook his head as if he tried to shake off the feelings. "Anyway, all that doesn't matter now. But my family…the church…what would they think if they heard about it?"

"They would respond just the way I did." At least, she hoped they would. "They'd know you couldn't possibly have done something like that—you would never harm a horse. It's impossible."

"You might be the exception. Other people aren't so generous." His face darkened. "I shouldn't have told you. Forget it."

The words sounded so familiar. That was what Elizabeth had said when she'd revealed her secret pain to Sally. Now Aaron was embarrassed, wondering why he'd told her something he didn't want anyone to know.

Sally couldn't help it. She had to touch him—just a gentle hand on his sleeve, but she could feel the warmth of his skin through the thin cotton. "I won't say anything. You can trust me."

Aaron swung toward her with an abrupt movement. Before she could identify the expression on his face, he pulled her into his arms. His lips found hers, and he held her as if he were a drowning man and she his only hope of saving.

No, she was the one who was drowning…in

overwhelming love and tenderness. Her palms pressed against the strong, flat muscles of his back as she responded to his kiss, feeling the deep need he had for caring.

How foolish she'd been, she thought through the haze that surrounded her, to ever say that what she'd felt before had been love. She'd never known anything like this, never even dreamed that she could feel this way.

Aaron's hand cupped her face so gently, so tenderly. He brushed a line of light kisses across her cheek and then put his cheek against hers.

"Aaron." She whispered his name. She wanted to stay here, in the warm circle of his arms, forever.

But as if the word had wakened him, Aaron let go of her so suddenly she nearly lost her balance. Groping, her hand found the edge of her desk and gripped it.

"I shouldn't have done it." He seemed to force the words out against his will. "This is wrong."

Sally looked at him steadily, willing him to see what she did. "It's only wrong if you don't feel what I do."

A spasm of pain reflected in his eyes. "I do.

You have to know that. What I feel now—I've never felt this way about anyone else. Ever."

Her heart began to beat again. "Well, then…"

"Don't, Sally." He made a sharp, cutting gesture with his right hand. "Don't you see? You're as real and solid as the rich earth and clean air of this place. I love you, but it's no good."

"Why?" Her desperation sounded in the word. She'd been given a taste of everything she could ever want, and now he was snatching it away.

He flung himself away from her. "It's no good because you can't leave. And I can't stay."

The words sliced into her heart like a knife. She shook her head in denial. "Why not? Why can't you stay? Since you've come back, you've fit in here as if you'd never gone away."

"I can't. You know as well as I do that I can't stay unless I'm prepared to be Amish again."

"Why not? You are Amish. You've never been anything else in your heart." Didn't he see that?

"No." The word was sharp. "I'd have to let everyone know what happened to me out there. I'd have to kneel in front of the whole of the Leit and confess what I've done." His quick anger flared in his face. "I can't. I won't have everyone looking at me and pitying me or condemning me. I should never have come back."

Sally pressed her hand against her chest as if she could keep her heart from breaking into pieces. He'd admitted that he loved her, but he wouldn't humble himself to claim her. He was still the boy she'd known…the one with the quick temper and the stubborn pride that wouldn't let him admit it when he'd done wrong.

He'd sacrifice their happiness for that pride, and she could do nothing, because only God could change his stubborn heart.

Chapter Eleven

Somehow Sally got through the next few days. At least she hadn't seen Aaron again, and she supposed that made it easier. No, nothing could actually make it easier. Staying busy just dulled the pain a little.

She glanced around her classroom, checking to see that all of her scholars were occupied in the reading she'd set for them at the end of the school day. Most of the heads were down, although she caught the gazes of one clock-watcher and two daydreamers. A look set them back to their assignment.

She'd formed the habit of this quiet time at the end of the day so that she could look back over the day's activities to see if any concerns had surfaced. In the midst of the busyness of all those children of different ages, something she ought to pay attention to slipped by. Now she could think it through and decide if action should be taken.

It was also a time when any student who was having a problem could come to her for extra help. No one had today, probably because they were excited about the auction coming up tomorrow. It was hard to focus on anything when they could hear the noises made by the parents who were setting up just outside the windows.

She rather wished someone had claimed her attention. Sitting here quietly it was only too easy to let her thoughts wander back a few days, to those moments when she'd stood in almost this spot and heard Aaron say that their love was impossible.

Restless, Sally rose and walked to the window, staring out and barely seeing the men who were putting up a canopy in case of rain for the auction. Aaron had said he loved her, and in the same breath, he'd claimed he couldn't sacrifice his pride for that love. Her heart twisted at the thought. That wasn't love.

Somehow she'd managed to cope, hiding her feelings and getting through the days as best she could. She'd even achieved a measure of peace by telling herself that God's will for Aaron was surely that he stay here.

If so, God would work it out. She could pray for him, and she did, but Aaron had to be the one to open his heart to hear God's will. No one else could do it for him.

A shuffle of feet behind her announced that someone thought it was dismissal time. She turned with a smile. "You may put your work in your desk now." She held up her hand for quiet. "If your family is here and wants you to stay and help, of course that's fine. If not, let's get lined up for dismissal."

They scurried to do as she asked. Those whose parents were outside assumed a self-satisfied look, but it didn't really matter whether parents were here today or not—everyone would show up tomorrow to help with the auction. After all, it was their school that would benefit. People cared about that…the whole church community as well as the parents who had children in the school.

By the time she got outside, quite a few people had gathered, most of them already busy.

"Teacher Sally!" Leah, looking ready to pounce, seemed to have been waiting on the porch, her arms filled with linens. "Can we start setting up inside for displaying the quilts and such?"

"For sure." Sally held the door. "Komm. We'll have to move some desks and chairs around to display them."

Leah hurried inside, waving several helpers to join her, and Sally followed them in. She'd best take a hand before someone decided to put her school supplies someplace where she'd never find them.

Staying busy setting up tables and pushing desks together was a good antidote to thinking about Aaron and wondering if he was among the outside helpers. They began spreading out handmade quilts and place mats.

"This baby quilt is wonderful." She picked up one in shades of palest pinks, greens and yellows that formed a block pattern. "Jessie should have this."

Leah smiled. "She does. That is, Rebecca and I gave her one just like it. Rebecca made them for the quilt shop, and Jessie raved over the pattern so much that we knew she'd love it for her little one."

"Perfect. You know my sister will soon have an addition to her family. I might have to bid on this one." Thinking of her sister, so far away, made her think of Mamm and Daad.

And of how much she longed for their steady presence and reassuring love right now.

"Your parents are staying to help out, ain't so?"

Of course Leah was well-informed on what the neighbors were doing. Secrets were hard to keep in the Amish community, and Sally clutched her own close to her heart. No one should know what she felt for Aaron, not now.

"Yah, they're eager to fuss over the new little one." She frowned slightly, remembering Daad's last call. "They like helping to get the new Amish church district started out there, I think. It's a big change from being here. You know they only have ten families?"

"I've heard that." Leah spread out a quilt with careful hands. "Still, ten families is a fine start, especially when most of them are young marrieds who will start having kinder. They'll need a school before they know it."

"Teacher Sally?" The call came from outside. "Where do you want the food stands?"

Leah grinned. "They'll put them where they always do, but you'd best go and direct them, so they can say they asked you."

Sally obediently went outside, giving a cautious look around for Aaron. She'd be bound to see him again soon, but she'd really like enough warning to be sure her armor was in place.

Daniel and his onkel Zeb were present, with Becky and her little brother helping to string a line from tree to tree to mark off space for car parking. There would undoubtedly be some Englisch neighbors come to bid on things, and no one wanted the cars mixed in with the horses and buggies.

But the rest of the King family was absent, and she wasn't sure whether she was relieved or saddened.

"Komm see what we're doing, Teacher Sally!" Becky called and waved.

"In just a minute." First she must meet with those setting up the various food stands.

Sure enough, each of them knew exactly where their stands went…in the same place they'd been the last time. But she solemnly agreed to each placement and expressed her gratitude for their cooperation.

Becky was still waving, so Sally made her way across the schoolyard.

"Very gut work," she said, looking from Becky to Zeb, who was helping her tie off a streamer. "Looks like you're planning on lots of folks with cars tomorrow."

"Sure enough," Zeb said. "It's going to be

a sunny day, and I've even heard the men at the feed mill talking about the sale. It'll be a gut sale, that's certain sure."

"I hope you're right. The roof repair took a bite out of the budget."

Zeb's leathery face split in a grin. "So Caleb keeps reminding us. He's bringing a wagonload of things later, and Jessie says she's making an extra batch of whoopie pies."

"That's wonderful kind of her, but she shouldn't be doing too much." Not so soon after having a new baby, she thought.

"Ach, there's no stopping her, but I made her promise to leave the icing. Becky and I will finish them when we get home."

Becky nodded. "I love making whoopie pies."

"And eating them," Timothy said, making them all laugh.

No mention of Aaron, so apparently he wasn't showing up to help, at least not today. She would not let herself feel disappointed.

Zeb nodded back toward the schoolhouse. "Looks as if your brother is looking for you."

Sure enough, Ben came hurrying toward her. She went to meet him, praying nothing was wrong to put him in such a rush. But he was smiling when he came up to her.

"You missed a call from Daad. He forgot about it being the day before the sale, or he'd have known you'd be here late. He says he's sorry not to talk to you, but he'll call back tonight after supper."

"That's gut. There's nothing wrong, is there?"

His grin reassured her. "He says Mamm thinks the boppli will be coming soon. He didn't know why she thinks that, because he says the first one is usually late."

"I'd guess Mamm knows more about it than he does. I think I'll go with her opinion." Happiness bubbled up at the thought of her little sister becoming a mammi. Impossible, that's what it seemed. She focused on Ben. "Did you tell Elizabeth?"

He stared at her. "Yah, for sure. Why wouldn't I? She's happy about it."

Was he trying to deny what was so obvious to her? Or did he really not see it? Sally bit her tongue to keep the words in. She'd promised Elizabeth she wouldn't say anything, so she couldn't. But the urge to give her brother a shaking had never been so strong.

Poor Elizabeth. Another baby in the family, and still none for her after six years. If Mammi were here...

Sally realized abruptly that it wasn't only

Elizabeth who needed to talk to Mammi right now, as close as she was to her mother-in-law. Sally needed it even more.

There was no one, no one at all, that she could talk to about her feelings for Aaron. The girls who had been so close during their teen years had moved on to marriage and children of their own. Much as she loved them, she couldn't talk to them. And she certain sure couldn't talk to Elizabeth about Aaron.

Mammi was the only person she might have confided in, and Mammi was far away and preoccupied with the coming baby. So she not only had to hold her secret to herself, she had to put on her usual upbeat face and never let anyone know.

Aaron arrived early at the schoolhouse the day of the auction with Daniel, since his brother had volunteered him to help get everything ready. Daniel nudged him as they pulled in.

"What's wrong with you? Still sleepy? Wishing you'd waited to come later with the others?"

"I'm fine." Aaron ground out the words, finding his brother's teasing more annoying than usual today. "You go see who needs help. I'll take care of the mare and the buggy."

Nodding, Daniel hopped down. "Don't put her next to that bad-tempered mare of Gus Albright's. Those two hate each other."

"Will do." In his opinion, Daniel's Queenie was the one with the bad temper, but it wouldn't do to say that to his brother, since Daniel had raised her since she was a filly.

Relieved to have an excuse for not joining the people who were hustling around the schoolyard, he took his time about the task. He knew perfectly well what had caused his shortness with his brother. He'd avoided Sally all week, but he couldn't possibly keep from seeing her today.

It hadn't been easy, doing without her. He'd missed her teasing smile and the flash of her dimple, to say nothing of the bright curiosity in her blue eyes and the glow of warmth and concern in her face. But it was for the best that he stay away from her.

He'd said too much, revealing his inner thoughts and torments in a way he'd have said was impossible. And after that kiss that had rocked him right down to the ground, what was there to do? He had no choice—he had to either ask Sally to marry him or to pretend it hadn't happened. And he couldn't ask her to marry him.

So there wasn't really a choice at all.

He couldn't deny that she'd known him only too well, though. She'd compared Mr. Winfield's quick temper to his own. She'd said he should give the man a second chance. She hadn't pointed out that he himself had been given a second chance by the community. She'd trusted he'd see that for himself.

It made too much sense to ignore, and he'd begun to feel as if it was the Lord rapping at his thoughts, urging him to take action. So he'd written to Albert Winfield.

No pleading. Just a simple telling of everything that had happened. He hadn't wanted to confess about his foolishness in trusting the wrong woman, but he'd told it all.

He hadn't asked for his job back…didn't even know if he wanted it. But he'd felt better when the letter was written and in the mail. Then it was too late to change his mind. Maybe Winfield would tear up the letter unread, but he'd done what he could.

When he rejoined his brother, he was immediately swept into helping set up the speaker system the auctioneer would be using. Isaiah Byler had been running auctions in Lost

Creek, Pennsylvania, ever since Aaron could remember. His reddish beard had plenty of gray in it now, and his voice might be a little weaker, but he was still master of the rapid-fire patter folks expected from an auctioneer. Aaron suspected some people came just to be entertained by him.

It took some time to have everything set up in the way Isaiah wanted it, but Isaiah finally nodded in satisfaction.

"I'm picky, ain't so? But we have to get it right, you know." He gave Aaron a friendly clap on the shoulder. "I don't have the volume I used to, so I need the help."

"Daniel says you still have the stamina you used to, though. According to him, you won't stop until every single thing finds a new home."

"Got to raise the money for the school, ain't so? Can't have the kinder running out of books and such." Isaiah glanced over Aaron's shoulder. "There's Teacher Sally coming now. That's never that spooky gelding Simon Stoltzfus bought at the livestock auction, is it?"

"That's Star, all right." He schooled himself to bear the sight of Sally, weaving her buggy competently through the busy grounds.

"Aaron had the training of him," Daniel put in. "Or retraining, I guess you'd say."

Isaiah grinned. "For sure any horse Simon trained or even picked out would need that. Never saw an Amishman so lacking in horse sense. But I'd have said that animal never could be trained. Too skittish by nature." He looked at Aaron with a tinge of respect in his face. "It's gut to see you developed your promise as a horseman."

"I worked with a harness racing outfit out west," he said, as briefly as possible.

"You know, I've got a two-year-old filly that needs training. Pretty flighty, and I haven't got the time or patience to work with her. Think you might be interested in taking her on?"

Aaron hesitated. He'd been on the verge of leaving for the past few days, but somehow he hadn't been ready to do it. Besides, he'd given his word to Bishop Thomas that he'd live by the Ordnung for a month. He couldn't back out now just because staying had become difficult. The reason for that had nothing to do with the Ordnung.

The lure of working with Isaiah's horse called to him—the greater the challenge, the better. And a lot could happen in three weeks.

"I'll give it a try, if you want. At least I can give you my opinion on her."

"Gut. Stop over any morning this week, and we'll see what you think." He looked around at the gathering crowd. "Looks like we're about ready to start. See you soon, yah?"

Aaron nodded. Like he'd told himself, a lot could happen in three weeks.

He and Daniel wandered through the crowd, taking a look at the items on display. Daniel was on the lookout for any tools he might be interested in, and Caleb, once he showed up, would have an eye out for farming implements. He'd been muttering something about a harrow when they'd left this morning.

As for him...well, there was nothing he needed in his footloose life, was there? Still, he ought to support the sale. He'd take a look through the toys and books. Maybe there'd be something Becky or Timothy might like. Or something for the new baby.

If...when he left, he'd like it if they had something to remember him by.

He turned to point something out to Daniel and nearly bumped into Sally. She looked as startled as he felt.

But it only lasted an instant, and then she was

back to her usual smiling self. "So, what are the two of you doing? Bidding on anything?"

"Still looking," he said, trusting he sounded normal. "Hope it's a great moneymaker for the school."

"Bound to be," Daniel said. "Look at the crowd. Nobody would dare leave without buying something. And it's brought Aaron benefit already. He's picked up work training another horse, thanks to you and Star."

"Thanks to us?"

"Yah. Isaiah spotted you driving Star this morning and decided Aaron was just the man he needed."

"That's wonderful gut. I'm glad we brought you some business already." It was said with a quick smile for Aaron. He was probably the only one who could tell that her smile wasn't quite as usual.

"We'll be sehr glad to get him out of the house again," Daniel teased. "He's been moping around bored as can be without seeing you and Star every day."

The color came up in Sally's cheeks, and Aaron felt like clouting his brother. He couldn't have said anything worse if he'd planned it ahead of time.

Before Aaron could come up with something to distract Daniel, it was done for him.

"That looks like a tool chest over there. I have to have a look." Daniel headed off, intent.

"I'm sorry." Aaron rushed the words off. "He didn't know... I mean, nobody suspects anything. I wouldn't talk about it."

"It's all right." The pink had washed out of her cheeks, leaving her looking a little pale. "I understand. Daniel would never say anything like that if he knew."

Sally's response was so heartfelt that it was a separate little barb in his heart. She understood. She always had, and she always would. That was what made this whole thing between them so hard.

She seemed to sense his inner struggle. "It's all right," she said, her soft words meant only for him. "We were friends first of all, and that doesn't change. We're still friends."

"Denke." He should be grateful that Sally was being sensible about the situation. So why should that annoy him at the same time? Was he mean enough to want her to show the world a broken heart?

Chapter Twelve

Sally leaned back in her spot at the kitchen table with a sigh of satisfaction. Supper had been a light meal of Elizabeth's homemade vegetable soup, and it had been just right after a long day spent at the school auction.

"I wouldn't be surprised if today was the best school auction we've had in years." She smiled at Ben and Elizabeth. "Thanks to all the support we had."

"Yah, it was gut. Caleb said he'd try to have the totals by tomorrow." Ben's gaze turned toward the harness that was slung over the back porch railing, clearly visible through the screen door.

"You can't wait to get that harness polished up," Elizabeth said, topping off his coffee. "I see you eyeing it. I think you men are even worse than women when it comes to finding a bargain."

"It's not for me," Ben protested. "It's chust what Daad needs for the pony cart. He wouldn't want me to pass it by when it's in such fine shape."

"I guess not." Elizabeth patted the fat brown teapot she'd found. "I never thought I'd find the perfect teapot. And so cheap, too."

Sally's lips curved. That was the great thing about a sale…everyone donated and then they all went home with something they needed. The school made money for repairs and equipment and, she hoped, some new books she'd had her eye on.

"I don't think there was a thing left at the end," she said. "Elizabeth's pies disappeared in no time at all. Folks knew something good when they saw it."

Elizabeth brightened, but only for a moment. Her gaze moved back to the back door, left open so they could hear the phone from the phone shanty. Daad had said he'd call tonight. Maybe he'd have news of Alice's baby.

Elizabeth would try to be happy for Alice. She *would* be happy. But Sally understood now how each new baby reminded her of her loss. She'd felt the same each time she'd seen a courting couple walking around the sale, eyes only for each other. Each glimpse had been a fresh pain in her heart for what could never be.

Sally had gotten up to put her dishes in the sink when they heard the sound they'd been waiting for. The phone rang, and since she was already on her feet, she beat Ben to the back door. They jostled each other, each trying to get to the phone shanty first.

Sally snatched up the receiver, edging Ben out by a step. "Hello. Daadi?"

Her father's deep voice boomed from the phone, and she held it so the others could hear.

"Gut news! Our Alice has a baby girl— chust as sweet and pretty as can be. They're both fine, thank the gut Lord."

Sally breathed a silent prayer of thankfulness. "That's wonderful. How much does the little one weigh? Does she have hair?"

Daad chuckled. "A little wisp of hair so light it's almost white. Mammi says it will darken up. And she weighs almost seven pounds."

"Tell them we're wonderful happy for them," Ben shouted into the receiver. Like Daad, he seemed to think yelling helped the telephone carry his message.

"Yah, yah, I will. Your mammi says to tell you all she misses you."

"We miss you, too, Daadi." They couldn't know how much Sally longed to have them near enough to confide in. "When will you be coming home?"

"As for that, I don't know. There's lots to be done here with getting the new church district organized. These young folks actually seem to appreciate having us old people around to advise them."

A whisper of concern ran along her nerves. Daadi almost sounded as if he were growing attached to that new place. He was always one who liked a challenge. Maybe he felt as if life here in Lost Creek had gotten stale.

"We need you here, too." She couldn't say more, much as she'd like to. That would be selfish. "So come back soon. Give our love to everyone."

Sally handed the phone over to Ben to say his goodbyes, trying not to let dismay get the upper hand. Maybe she was being selfish, but if Mamm and Daad decided to stay out there, what would become of her?

Her gaze caught the expression on Elizabeth's face, and she felt ashamed of her own self-centeredness. Elizabeth was struggling with a far deeper pain, and Ben, being more obtuse than usual, didn't even recognize it.

She slipped her arm around Elizabeth's waist as she turned toward the kitchen. "It's getting chilly out here now. Let's get inside and try out that new teapot of yours. Want to split one of those whoopie pies we brought home?"

Elizabeth seemed grateful to have something else to focus on. "Yah, I'd like fine to give it a try. Denke, Sally."

They went inside, closing the door against the evening chill. Ben stopped inside the door and stretched. "Ach, what an end to a busy day, ain't so? We had a wonderful gut sale, and our little Alice has a new baby girl. Quite a day."

"Yah, it was." Sally sent him a warning glare, but he didn't seem to get the message.

"Sounds like he and Mamm are really enjoying life out there. Could be they'll decide to stay."

She'd hoped she was reading too much into Daad's comments. But if even Ben, obtuse as he was, had noticed it, it could be real.

Elizabeth turned away from the kettle and came to put her arm around Sally's waist in much the same gesture Sally had used. "Don't worry about it. I think they'll be eager to get home before long. And if they don't, you know you always have a home with us."

Naturally that was what she'd say. It was automatic in any Amish family. But Sally heard the real caring that underlay the words, and though it wasn't the life she would have wanted, she was comforted.

The next week went quietly for Aaron. He started working with the new filly, and between that and the farm work, he kept busy. But not quite busy enough, since he found he was thinking of Sally too much.

Still, it was better not to see her. Better for both of them, he felt sure. But it was a long week.

Worship was held the following Sunday morning at the home of a distant cousin of the King family, Elijah Esh. That meant that Aaron and his brothers arrived early to help with the final setup for worship.

Elijah and Mary had a large prefab shed that they used when they hosted worship, and it was easy to see that the family had been hard at work removing the equipment that usually lived in the shed and scrubbing the space until it shone.

The church wagon was pulled up next to

the shed, and Aaron joined Daniel and Onkel
Zeb in pulling the benches out and carrying
them inside. Timothy scurried along behind
them, eager to help, while Caleb took Jessie
and the baby into the kitchen to wait until time
for worship. Becky marched along with them,
proudly toting the diaper bag.

Onkel Zeb grabbed one end of a bench before Aaron could beat him to it. "I told Caleb
to wait and bring Jessie and the baby a bit
later. It's a mite cold out this early for such a
little one."

"I'm sure Jessie will enjoy a quiet gossip
with Mary in a warm kitchen before everyone comes flooding in." Aaron swung his end
around so that he was the one to walk backward.

"Yah, I guess so." Zeb shook his head at
the teenage boy who tried to take his end of
the bench. "Ach, I'm not that old yet. Aaron,
you remember Elijah and Mary's oldest boy,
Adam, yah?"

The boy grinned at him. "I've changed
since you last saw me." His voice was as low
as his father's.

"You have. I'd say the least Onkel Zeb could
do is let you carry a bench, given how big
you are."

"Yah, that's so. Timothy and I can take it, ain't so, Timmy?"

Timothy's small chest expanded. "Sure thing. Let us, Onkel Zeb."

Zeb handed it over. "What can I do, with two young men eager to help?"

Relieved, Aaron saw Onkel Zeb move off to greet Elijah's father. Always so eager to carry his share of the load, that was Zeb, but it was time he took things a little easier.

And if you leave again? The small voice in the back of his mind asked the question. *Who will be around to lend a helping hand until Timothy and his baby brother are old enough to step in?*

He didn't want to go where that question led him. He hadn't even thought about things like that before his world had fallen apart around him, and he felt a flicker of shame. It was one thing to pursue his call to the outside world and another thing entirely to cut off the family he'd left behind.

That realization clung to his mind like a cobweb he couldn't wipe away. Why had he given so little thought to them?

At first it had been a necessity, he knew. If he'd thought too much about his family and his home, he'd have given up and gone home.

Those first months had been hard, and it was only his pride that had kept him from heading back.

Eventually he'd pushed his family so far back in his mind that he'd barely thought of them at all. There'd been nothing and no one to remind him that he'd once had another life.

Now…now he couldn't forget. If and when he left again, there would still be an unbreakable cord attaching him to this place and these people. And to Sally.

Helping Adam arrange the benches kept his body occupied, but it didn't do a thing to stop his thoughts. Images of her tossed and tumbled through his mind… Sally laughing, Sally pensive and even Sally looking at him with her blue eyes filled with love.

How could he leave, knowing he'd never see her again? But how could he stay, seeing her and knowing she'd never be his?

Once the service began, Aaron forced himself to concentrate on the songs and prayers. At first it was difficult, but he found his agitated thoughts mellowed by the long slow notes of the songs. His mind automatically made the adjustment to the High German that was used in worship and scripture. He found the familiar words of the readings resonated, waking his mind to their meaning.

Odd, how he'd have said he'd forgotten all this during his years away. It wasn't forgotten; it had simply been stored temporarily, ready to come back the moment he needed it.

The longer sermon was given by the youngest of the ministers, a boy he remembered from school, only a few years older than he was. He'd never have said that Jacob Beiler had it in him to be a minister, but the call of God fell without the intervention of anyone else. God had chosen Jacob, and he'd grown into the job, it seemed.

When the service had ended and the tables had been set up, he found himself sitting across from Ben. Aside from a little initial uneasiness the first time they'd met after he'd asked Aaron about his relationship with Sally, Ben had gone back to his usual manner. Today he was even a little more animated than usual.

"Did you hear our news?" he asked around a large bite of sandwich. "Our Alice has had a baby girl."

"No, I didn't know." He'd guess Sally was relieved if that meant that her parents would soon be coming home. "Your mamm and daad must be happy."

"Ach, wonderful happy. Daadi called us last night, and he couldn't stop talking. Seems like she's the prettiest baby girl he's ever seen, by the sounds of it."

If the birth of a new niece made Ben think of his own childless home, he didn't let it show. And since Ben wasn't subtle enough to hide his feelings, Aaron would guess that his happiness was genuine.

He'd guess Elizabeth might be feeling differently. Sally had given him the idea that she was struggling when it came to that subject.

It seemed a shame, given how many unwanted babies there were in the world, that good people like Elizabeth and Ben should be childless.

Ben turned away to greet Bishop Thomas, who'd stopped at the end of the table, and regale him with their news. After congratulations and best wishes for the family, the bishop asked the question that Aaron had been wondering.

"Does this mean we'll have your mamm and daad back with us soon?"

Ben's plain, open face clouded over. "I don't know. Seems like they've really gotten involved in helping that new community get on its feet. There aren't so many Amish down in that part of southern Ohio, from what Daad says."

The bishop didn't offer an opinion, but then, that wasn't his way. He rested his hand on Ben's shoulder for a moment. "You'll tell them we're missing them, yah?"

Ben nodded and then turned away to answer a question about Alice from the woman who'd just put a full serving plate on the table. That left Bishop Thomas free to turn his attention to Aaron, who began to wish himself elsewhere.

"I've been hearing about you, Aaron."

It swept into his mind to wonder who'd been reporting on him to the bishop before he realized Bishop Thomas was smiling.

"Something gut, I hope."

"Ben says he had his doubts that gelding of Sally's was even trainable, but I hear you've got him behaving like a lamb."

Aaron's face relaxed. "I wouldn't say Star was exactly lamblike, but I don't think Sally will have any more trouble with him."

"You always did have a gift where horses were concerned."

He'd said what everyone did, and Aaron realized that coming from the bishop, the fact gratified him. Whatever else folks said about him, there was at least that positive thing.

"Star just needed retraining, that's all. Some folks skip past the fundamentals when it comes to horses."

"Some folks skip past the fundamentals when it comes to a lot of things," Bishop Thomas said. "It never does work out, not in the long run. We just have to go back to the beginning—to the things we learned first."

He gave Aaron that characteristic pat on the shoulder and moved off before Aaron could respond. He sat still for a moment, pondering those words.

Had the bishop been thinking of faith when he'd said that? Somehow that seemed to echo his feelings when he'd slipped back into the familiar worship without needing to consider it. Those, he supposed, were the beginning things—the things that a person knew in his heart without struggling.

He wasn't sure how long he'd have sat there, lost in thought, but one of the teenage girls who'd been pressed into service swept his plate out from in front of him. He realized that everyone else was getting up, so he followed suit. He'd have to leave deep thinking for another time.

No one was in any hurry to clean up and get back on the road except perhaps for those teenage girls. They were probably eager to finish their work so they could gather in giggling groups, eyeing the boys who tended to talk a little louder and gesture a little more broadly when the girls were watching. He smiled, remembering what it felt like to be one of them, so caught up in what your peers thought that you didn't have room for anything else.

"Have some dessert?" Sally appeared next to him, carrying a tray with various kinds of cake and pie slices. "The lemon squares are all gone, but there's plenty of chocolate cake."

"Thanks." He picked up a slab of chocolate cake with what looked like caramel icing. If Sally could behave normally around him, the least he could do was follow suit. "I hear you have a new little niece."

Her smile sparkled. "A beautiful girl, so we hear. I wish I could go and see her. Maybe over Thanksgiving, when we have a few days off school."

"Your mamm will be eager to head back

and see how she's grown by then." It occurred to him that it might not be the most tactful thing to say, especially when a tiny wrinkle appeared between her brows.

"If they've come home by then. I keep fearing they'll say they've decided to stay out there."

"Surely not. Their lives have been here. To say nothing of their other kinder."

"I hope you're right." She seemed to shake herself. "That sounds selfish."

"But understandable." He couldn't help thinking about that promise he'd once made to marry her when she grew up. If Sally were married, she wouldn't have to worry about living with her brother and his wife for good.

But there was no sense in thinking about something he'd already decided was impossible. "If they stayed out there, are you thinking that you might join them? Their community will probably need a teacher."

Now, that sounded as if he were trying to get rid of her. Why was he being so awkward around her?

"No, I won't do that." Sally spoke with certainty. "I know where I belong, and it's here."

Simple, it seemed, to her. Sally knew

where she belonged. Too bad he couldn't say the same.

She started to turn away, and he spoke abruptly.

"There's something I ought to tell you."

She looked back at him, blue eyes questioning.

"What we talked about…about why I left my job. I started thinking about what you said, and I decided I should write to Winfield. Just to tell him what happened from my side."

"And did you?"

He gave a rueful smile. "It wasn't the easiest thing I've ever written, but I did it. Then I wanted to snatch it back from the mailbox a half a dozen times, but I didn't. I actually felt relieved when I saw the mail truck carry it down the road."

She nodded, but her face, usually so expressive, didn't give away her feelings. "Are you hoping he offers you your job back again?"

"No, not exactly. I don't know that I'd want to go back. But after what you said… Well, I couldn't just leave it."

"I see." Sally managed a slight smile, but there was something more in her eyes, something he didn't quite understand. "I'm glad you were able to put your pride in your pocket when it came to making things right with Mr. Winfield."

She turned and was gone, carrying her tray like a shield, before he could respond.

Once again he was left thinking, wondering and trying to puzzle out the meaning behind her words.

Chapter Thirteen

Sally should have gotten used to not seeing Aaron waiting for her at the paddock when she got home from school. He had finished his job and moved on. That was all anyone needed to know. Sally drove Star up to the hitching rail outside the barn, wishing she could convince herself.

No, she didn't want that. She wouldn't give up those moments of closeness. That was all she'd have.

When she'd walked away from Aaron the previous day after church, she'd told herself that was an end to it. She didn't have to be hit with a two-by-four to know when something was over.

She slid down from the buggy and began to remove the harness from Star. Aaron had told her more than he realized when he'd said that he'd written to his former employer to defend himself. He'd been willing to humble himself for a man she'd never seen, but not for her. That said everything.

And she'd best take her time about unharnessing, or she'd be walking into the house with a face that would give her away to anyone as sharp as Elizabeth. She had to stop thinking about Aaron, or she'd have half the church feeling sorry for her while the other half considered that it served her right.

Well, maybe not the second part of it. There might be a few people who still blamed her for jilting Fred, but not many. Not when he was so obviously happily married. And the father of twins, no less.

But she still had no desire to let folks know how she felt. What happened would stay between her and Aaron, and it was obvious that Aaron had successfully put it behind him.

Sally hung the harness on its rack and proceeded to brush Star down. She hadn't driven that far and the day was cool, so it wasn't really necessary, but she found the smooth, even movements as soothing as Star did. Bending, she checked Star's hooves. Daadi had taught her to drive, not entirely trusting Ben to do it, and he was always particular about how the horses were shod when they were used on the hard road surface.

Everything seemed to conspire to remind her of things she'd rather not think about. If Mammi and Daadi did decide to relocate out to Ohio, she'd have to find a tactful way of making a change in her living arrangements. It would be unheard of for a woman her age to live alone, but whether Ben and Elizabeth moved back to their own house or more liking stayed here, they'd expect her to live with them. Maybe they'd agree that she could have the grossdaadi haus, next to the farmhouse. At least that would give her a little more privacy. And Ben and Elizabeth might well feel they wanted privacy, as well.

When she walked back to the house, she gave a considering look at the grossdaadi haus, empty for several years now. She and Mamm always kept it clean and tidy for company, and it wouldn't require any changes for her to move in. The living room and kitchen downstairs and two bedrooms and bath upstairs would be more than enough space for her.

With that to occupy her mind, Sally could push the memory of Aaron's kiss far enough back to ignore it, at least. One day she'd get over him.

She went inside and found Elizabeth peeling potatoes for supper.

"Just let me wash up, and I'll do those." She lathered her hands and wrists thoroughly, not wanting to carry the scent of horse into their supper.

"Denke, Sally." Elizabeth surrendered the peeler to her. "That would be a help."

Sally darted a glance at her sister-in-law. Elizabeth sounded as if she were trying hard to be cheerful, but other than that, she could see no signs that Elizabeth was feeling depressed. If Mammi were here, she thought for the hundredth time, she'd know what to do about Elizabeth.

She hesitated, trying to think of a neutral topic of conversation, but Elizabeth saved her the trouble.

"The school auction was wonderful gut, ain't so? I heard that was the most money we've raised at one auction in years."

It seemed to Sally that Elizabeth was watching her, trying to measure her feelings. Maybe Elizabeth was checking her for signs of depression, just as she did with Elizabeth. The thought amused her for a moment, but she wondered what it might mean.

"Yah, that was a blessing for sure, especially with the cost of the new roof."

"You'll be able to get some new books. And I told Ben we should see about replacing those bookshelves that got wet when the roof leaked."

Sally blinked. Elizabeth had expressed more interest in the school in the past few minutes than she had all year. It was almost as if she thought Sally needed cheering up, or...

Then she got it. Elizabeth always kept an eye on her when Aaron was around. She had probably been watching when Sally had stalked away from Aaron yesterday after church. So she hadn't hidden her emotions as well as she'd thought.

"Star has been going fine for you since Aaron finished with her. He does a gut job with the horses, I guess." Elizabeth must be concerned if she were willing to go to the extent of complimenting Aaron. Sally didn't know whether to laugh or cry.

"Yah, he has." She took a breath, trying to sort out the confusion in her own mind. And then the words spilled out before she could censor them. "I'm glad Aaron had time to train Star before he goes away again."

"Is he going away?"

"I think so." She choked up suddenly, turning her face so that Elizabeth couldn't see her expression.

Her sister-in-law came close, gently taking the peeler from her hand. "It will be all right." She stroked Sally's back, patting her the way Mammi would. "It will."

A jumble of thoughts crowded her mind, and out of it one thing became clear. She accused Aaron of being prideful, but wasn't she doing the same thing, loath to show Elizabeth her suffering? She was trying to hold on to her own pride instead of practicing the humility that was a cornerstone of Amish faith.

She turned into Elizabeth's arms, feeling them soft around her, hearing the words of comfort that fell on her like a gentle murmur of peace. She could surrender her own self-will, but it was one thing no person could do for another. As long as Aaron clung to his pride, there could be no future for them.

Eventually she was cried out. She drew back, mopping her eyes, trying to smile. "I got you all wet."

"Ach, that's nothing." She pressed a fresh tea towel into Sally's hand. "Use that."

With a shaky laugh, she complied. "I'm sorry. You tried to warn me, but I didn't listen."

"Ach, I should have saved my breath. No one in love wants to hear it." She paused and then added, "Is there no chance he'll stay?"

"Very little." Sally sucked in a breath. Her eyes burned and her face felt hot, but the hard knot in her chest had dissolved. "I'll be all right. I have plenty to keep me busy."

She didn't really believe that, but it might help Elizabeth to hear it.

"About that..." Elizabeth stopped, as if struggling with the words. "I have been thinking about that special doctor. I... I would be afraid to go myself. But if you will go with me, I can do it."

Sally nearly burst into tears again. Was Elizabeth trying to distract her? Or had she somehow, through her suffering, become what her sister-in-law needed just now? She didn't really need to know why—just to accept that some good had come from suffering.

She wrapped her arms around Elizabeth, holding her tight. "I would love to. We'll call the doctor and set it up."

A few tears slipped out then, but it didn't matter. Elizabeth was crying, too, but for both of them, they were tears of hope.

Aaron knelt beside the front porch steps, giving the railing a tentative wiggle. Sure enough, it was loose, and they couldn't risk someone getting hurt.

As he opened the toolbox, he found he was glancing toward the mailbox. Here it was Thursday, and all week he'd been first to check the mail just in case he heard back from Albert Winfield. It was too soon, he knew that. And even if he heard the best possible response, he didn't know that he'd be comfortable returning to his job. Still, he wanted to know.

Small wonder he wasn't very good at being Amish. He seemed to be totally missing in the traditional Amish virtues like patience and humility.

He caught a glimpse of movement at the Stoltzfus farm from the corner of his eye and resolutely looked away. Seeing Sally would only remind him of how much he missed being around her. And made it doubly certain that staying away was the right choice.

If he couldn't offer her marriage, it was

much better not to see her at all. Unfortunately, he couldn't block out the image that was in his mind. That clung, persistent, no matter what he did. It changed, though. Sometimes it was Sally laughing, but more often it was Sally with her eyes filled with love.

Enough. He focused on the porch railing. He'd need to reset one of the posts that had worked its way loose and then check each separate paling.

He'd been working for probably fifteen minutes when he realized he had an audience. Becky and Timothy had joined him, looking on silently. Seeing he'd noticed them, they smiled, Becky with that sweet tilt of her head and Timothy with the wide grin that seemed likely to split his face.

"We didn't make any noise. Mammi said we shouldn't bother you when you were working," Becky explained.

"We didn't bother you, did we, Onkel Aaron?" Timothy gave him a hopeful look.

"No bother at all," he said. "I'm just fixing the porch railing. It wiggles, and we wouldn't want Mammi to fall when she comes out."

"Can we help?" Becky clasped her hands in front of her, and Timothy looked eagerly at the hammer.

"Suppose you hold this for me." He tried to be tactful, but he didn't think he was ready to turn Timothy loose with a hammer.

He positioned one of them at each end of the railing, safely out of range of the tools while he went on with his work. "Did you have a gut week at school, Becky?"

"The week isn't over yet, Onkel Aaron." Her face was serious, as if he might not know that. "We still have tomorrow, and that's spelling test day."

He grinned at her solemn correction. "Okay, other than the spelling test, was it gut?"

She nodded. "I got a star on my arithmetic paper. And I studied my spelling words, so I think I know them all."

Timothy watched her, a little apprehensive. "You have a test every week?"

"Every week," she intoned. Then she smiled. "It's not hard. You just print the words after Teacher Sally says them."

"You'll do fine when you get to school," Aaron assured Timothy.

"Yah. And Teacher Sally is the best teacher ever. Everybody says so," Becky put in. Then she paused, staring at him. "Are you mad at Teacher Sally, Onkel Aaron?"

The smile he'd had vanished abruptly.

"No, I'm not." He should leave it there, but he couldn't. "What would make you think that I'm mad at her?"

"She never comes around," Timothy said.

So they'd noticed, and they had been talking about it.

"And you don't go over there anymore." Becky jerked her head toward the Stoltzfus farm.

Aaron did his best not to let his face betray him. He pounded in a nail and reached for another. "I went to the Stoltzfus place every day when I was training Star, you know that, yah? Now that he's doing so well, he's graduated. I don't need to work with him anymore, and I'm working with a new horse."

A quick glance told him they both understood, but still, they looked disappointed. What was going on in their little heads?

"Look." He gave the railing a shake, showing them that it stood firm. "We fixed it, and you were gut helpers. Denke."

Timothy grinned. "I'm going to tell Daadi that I helped." He raced off at his usual run.

Becky squatted down and helped him put the tools away. She fingered a nail before dropping it in its compartment. "You know how to fix lots of things, don't you?"

It was nice to have someone looking at him as if he had all the answers. "Not as much as Onkel Daniel, I guess. But this wasn't a hard job."

"It was important. You said so nobody would fall. That's important."

He puzzled over that, wondering again what was in her mind. "Yah, I guess it's always important to keep people safe."

"Then you can fix the railing at school. It's wiggly just like this one was and somebody might get hurt. You can come tomorrow after school, and I'll stay and help you." She finished with a satisfied expression.

"I… I don't know." What he did know for sure was that he shouldn't go and see Sally, especially not at the place where he'd kissed her. "Maybe we should ask Onkel Daniel to do it. Or your daadi. He's on the school board."

"No, you please, Onkel Aaron. You'll let me help. They might say I'm too little. Please, please, please?"

She had the wheedling down pat. He knew perfectly well that Jessie would correct her if she heard it. He also knew that he wasn't immune to that pleading look.

He hesitated, weakening for reasons he

didn't want to analyze. Finally he nodded. "All right. Tomorrow after class is over. I'll be there, and we can walk home together afterward."

Chapter Fourteen

The quiet time at the end of the school day on Friday seemed to drag even more than it usually did. For the sake of her scholars, Sally couldn't show any sign of impatience, but she felt it. Silence gave her too much time to think.

This had felt like the longest week of her life. If she'd thought the pain in her heart would become easier to bear by now, she'd been wrong. She would heal, of course, given time. She'd be able to take joy in the routine moments of her life. But the hole in her heart where Aaron had been would never change.

The only bright spot of the week had been Elizabeth's agreement to see the specialist. She still wasn't quite sure what had done it. Did the suffering Sally had experienced con- vince her sister-in-law that she could understand? Did it form a shared bond? She didn't know, but she was thankful. Now all she could do was pray that their appointment next week would bring good results for Elizabeth and Ben.

A glance at the schoolroom clock told her it was time at last, and a look at her scholars made her laugh. They'd been watching the clock even more closely than she had.

"Yah, it's dismissal time. Put everything away please, and then you may get your jackets and line up by the door."

She followed the rush to the coatroom, knowing her watchful eye would ensure that the older students helped the young ones instead of rushing past them. Once they were all lined up she opened the door, standing by it to receive the goodbyes from each one.

"Goodbye, Teacher Sally." It was repeated by each scholar, and she was careful to give each one a warm smile. She'd never want a child to leave at the end of the school day without knowing that she treasured him or her, regardless of what had happened that day.

When the last one had passed her, she stepped out to the porch, as well...and nearly ran into Aaron.

For an instant her breath was gone, and she

could only stare at him, unable to speak. After too long, she got control of herself.

"Aaron. Are you here to walk home with Becky?"

He nodded, his face carefully expressionless. "I am, but first I'm ordered to fix a loose porch railing."

"Ordered? By whom? I was going to ask Ben to do it this weekend."

Aaron shot a look at Becky. "It was Becky's idea. She saw me doing the job at the farmhouse and thought I should make myself useful."

Sally eyed Becky with a certain amount of suspicion and found her looking from her teacher to her uncle and back again. She'd have to put the best possible face on it, but she certainly hoped Aaron didn't think she was behind it.

"Denke. It's kind of you."

Aaron squatted, checking the railing with deliberation. "Doesn't look bad. Becky and I will have it ready to go in a couple of minutes, ain't so, Becky?"

The child nodded. "Teacher Sally can help, too, can't she?"

Aaron's lips tightened slightly. "I don't think…"

"I'll just get my schoolwork ready to go,"

she said, and vanished before he could complete the thought.

It only took a moment to prepare the work she'd intended to take home with her, but she lingered in the schoolroom, not wanting Aaron to think she was eager to watch him work. Only when the hammering ceased did she venture back out again.

"Finished already?" She kept her voice even and pleasant—the way she'd speak to any parent who'd stopped by to help.

"Just about." He gave the railing a shake. "It shouldn't give you any more problems. I'll just clean up, and we'll be on our way."

"I'm on my way to harness Star. I'll give you a ride back." She could hardly fail to offer, no matter how dangerous it was to her heart to be with him.

"I'll help with the harness," Becky said, and was off like a shot.

Managing a smile, Sally followed. Becky wasn't tall enough to put the harness on, but she'd find something for the child to do.

Star seemed eager to be going home, and he stood quietly while they hitched him to the buggy. Sally led him around the school to the front with Becky patting him and whispering to him the whole time, fingering the harness.

"Here we are." She stopped by the porch to find Aaron closing his toolbox. "All ready to go."

Sally focused on the buggy rather than Aaron, her hand tightening on the line as she swung herself up. In an instant Star reared, jostling the buggy. Her hand slipped and she was falling, seeing the ground rush up to meet her.

She landed hard on her right shoulder, still clutching the books she'd held. The fall jarred her so that for a moment she couldn't think. Then Becky cried out, and Aaron rushed to her, kneeling and putting his arms around her.

"Sally!" It was nearly a cry. "Are you all right? Don't try to move."

She tried to speak, but she couldn't. She could only look at Aaron's face so close to hers and the love in his eyes turned her bones to jelly.

Struggling to control his feelings, Aaron held Sally gently, relieved to see that her gaze, fixed on him, seemed normal. "Easy, don't try to move too fast. Where does it hurt?"

She blinked several times, breaking eye contact, and seemed to be assessing how she felt. She moved a little, wincing slightly.

"My shoulder is sore, but I don't think anything is broken."

His pulse slowed, steadying, and he helped her sit up, relinquishing his hold on her reluctantly. "Take it slow and easy. I'll help you get up."

Sally nodded. Biting her lip and leaning on his arm, she got to her feet. When he let go she swayed, and he put a steadying hand on her elbow.

"Let's get you over to the step where you can sit down. Then I'll deal with the horse." He glared at Star, and the animal shook himself and kicked again.

They moved slowly to the steps, and he had to forcibly resist the urge to pick Sally up in his arms and carry her. He didn't have the right to do so. He didn't have any rights where Sally was concerned, and he had to remember it.

Sally relaxed with a sigh when she was seated on the steps. "I'm all right." Her gaze went past him to Becky, who was still weeping. "Becky, will you pick up my books and papers, please? That would be a big help."

Sniffling and nodding, Becky stooped and began collecting them. Seeing her safely away from the horse and buggy, Aaron approached Star.

"Settle down now," he murmured. "It's just me. You remember me, yah?"

Star tossed his head fretfully, but stopped kicking.

Still murmuring soothing words, Aaron began stroking the lathered neck. Star had worked himself into a nervous state—that was certain. But why?

"There now. What's wrong with you today? Nothing here to be scared of."

He glanced at Sally. She'd be losing faith in his ability with horses the way things were going. She sat on the step, leaning a little to one side, and she had her arm around Becky, soothing the child in much the same manner as he tried to soothe the horse.

What on earth had caused Star to lose his head that way? He couldn't see anything around that might have frightened the animal. Besides, with his blinders on, he could only see what was in front of him.

He moved his hand toward Star's shoulder, and a shiver went over the horse's skin like a warning.

"Hush, now, don't be foolish."

He looked back at Sally again, seeing Becky

staring at her with such devotion and love that it shone from her face. His heart seemed to turn over.

"You'll be wishing I'd never touched this animal to begin with," he said, trying to distract his thoughts from what he wanted to say.

"Teacher Sally doesn't think that," Becky said, rushing the words, her hands clasped tightly. "She couldn't."

"That's right." Sally patted her. "It's all right."

Aaron frowned. What was going on with Becky? Surely the sight of her teacher falling shouldn't upset her this much, at least now that she knew Sally was all right.

His hand moved along the shoulder, brushing against the strap of the harness. Star exploded again, rearing and kicking, his head tossing. Aaron caught the headstall, holding it firmly, trying not to think about those horseshoes connecting with his body.

"Stoppe. Are you ferhoodled? What's wrong with you?" Aaron fought to keep a controlled tone, not wanting to make matters worse.

Under his hands, Star settled, but he shivered all over and his ears flicked nervously.

"It's my fault!" The words came in a wail from Becky, and he spun around to stare at her.

"What are you talking about?" he demanded, but Becky only cried louder.

Sally sent him a reproving glance. "Hush, now, Becky. Don't be afraid. Just tell us what you think you did."

Becky sniffled, shivering just as Star had. Then the words spilled out. "Under the harness." She pointed a shaking finger. "There. I did it. I put a thorn from the rosebush under the strap."

Aaron's gaze met Sally's. He moved slowly, resting his palm on Star's shoulder near the harness. Star shuddered. He inched his hand along, slipping his fingers under the harness. And had to mind his tongue when he felt the sharp prick of a thorn.

Still moving deliberately, he eased the irritant out, alert for any sign of trouble from Star. But the horse seemed to know that Aaron was helping him, standing perfectly still as the thorny twig came clear. Aaron smoothed his hand along under the harness to make sure he'd gotten it all.

Star visibly relaxed. Whickering softly, he turned his head toward Aaron. Aaron patted him, murmuring soothing words while his mind spun. Caleb should be the one to cope with his daughter's behavior, but it looked as if this landed on him.

But Sally was already coping. She cupped Becky's face in her hands. "Komm, now, Becky. You must tell us why. You're not a child to be mean to an animal."

"No, no." Distraught, Becky shook her head vehemently. "I didn't know it would hurt Star so much. I just thought it would make him misbehave a little."

Sally looked toward Aaron, as if asking if he wanted to take over. But he didn't. Sally was obviously more capable than he was in this situation. He shook his head slightly.

"You wanted Star to misbehave? Why?"

Becky had been answering readily, but now she seemed to get stuck. Her cheeks grew red, and her lips pressed together. Then she put her hands over her face, hiding it.

Sally pulled the hands away, her touch gentle. "You have to answer, Becky. Why did you do it?"

Becky glanced from side to side, as if looking for a way out. Then she stared at her hands, clasping them tight in her lap.

"We… Timothy and me…we wanted to have…to have Teacher Sally for our aunt."

She rushed the last few words, eager to get them out. "But Onkel Aaron hasn't even been to see you all week. He said it was because he'd finished training Star. So I thought that if Star needed more training, you would get back together again."

She felt silent, still staring at her hands. Aaron moved to her side, not knowing what to say, and certainly not wanting to look at Sally. Finally he sighed and sat down next to Becky on the step.

Heaven only knew what Sally was thinking now. And he was going to have to make Becky see...

But again Sally, with that quick perception of hers, anticipated him. "Becky, you know that what you did was wrong, don't you?"

Becky nodded, shuddering. "I hurt Star. That was wrong."

He thought for a moment she'd say that she hadn't meant to hurt the horse, but she didn't. This little niece of his was taking responsibility for herself.

"You must understand that grown-up people have to decide things like marriage for themselves." Sally paused, and he realized how difficult this must be for her. It wasn't fair of him to let her carry the burden.

"That's right." He put his arm around Becky. "Getting married to someone isn't something you decide all in a hurry or because you spent some time together. You can't make that happen for other people."

Was it his imagination, or did Sally wince at that? He rushed on, not sure he wanted to know.

"Now I think it's time we went home." He glanced at Sally. "It might be best if I drive Star. All right?"

She nodded and bent to gather up her school materials, not looking at him. He ought to say something to make this better, but he couldn't, because there wasn't anything.

Sally put her materials in the buggy and then lifted Becky up, urging her over into the middle of the seat. She'd put a child in the center in any event for safety's sake, but right now she needed Becky as a buffer between her and Aaron.

She climbed up and settled herself, preparing to endure the trip home in Aaron's company. Just when she thought the hurt couldn't get any worse, it did.

The humiliating thing was the reflection that she'd been obvious enough about her feelings that the children saw it. Shame washed over her. That should never have happened. It violated everything she believed about the relationship between teacher and scholars.

Aaron had to share the responsibility, too, and he probably realized that. Regardless, she had to be responsible for her own behavior. She certainly couldn't control his.

They rode along in silence, each occupied by his or her own thoughts. Finally she shook herself loose of her preoccupation with her feelings and glanced across the buggy seat.

Aaron was stone-faced, giving nothing away. He looked like the man he'd been that first time she saw him as an adult—the day he came home.

It hurt too much, and she switched her gaze to Becky. Poor Becky. Sympathy swept over her. The child sat with her head hanging, her hands clasped together in her lap. She had to do something about Becky.

Putting an arm around Becky, she snuggled her close. Becky looked up, startled, and then relaxed against her, the tight look vanishing from her face.

"Look how nicely Star is going along now. I think that means he forgives us, don't you?"

Becky shot a glance toward her uncle. "Maybe. I hope so."

Sally wanted to poke him in the ribs, but she didn't dare. She stared at him so intensely that she thought he couldn't help but feel it.

Whether he did or not, Aaron roused himself. "Yah, I'm sure of it. He's a gut boy. He won't hold it against anybody. An extra carrot tonight, and he'll forgive anything, ain't so?"

She nodded, giving Becky a squeeze. "He's greedy, all right. I'll make sure he knows the extra carrot is from you."

At last Becky smiled. Without moving away from Sally, she reached across to take Aaron's hand, and they traveled along toward home, linked across the seat.

Sally's heart ached with the realization of how much Becky was going to miss her uncle when he left. Aaron obviously cared about her and Timothy, too. Didn't he see how much he meant to his family? Since he'd been back, he'd fitted right into the family, secure in his proper place.

Or was that wishful thinking on her part?

They rounded the bend in the lane that brought the two farms into view, and Becky bounced on the seat.

"Look. There's a car in front of our house. Who can it be?"

They looked where she was pointing. It meant nothing to Sally, but Aaron's whole body seemed to freeze. "I know." His voice had changed. "It's someone for me." He glanced at Sally and then quickly away. "It's the man I used to work for."

It was as if a giant hand had clutched her heart. Not now. It was too soon. She wasn't ready.

But she'd never be ready for Aaron to go away again.

"I thought I might get a letter. I never expected him to come here." Apprehension was plain in his voice.

"He wouldn't have come if he were still angry with you." The impulse to reassure him was stronger even than her regret. "You know that."

Aaron looked back at the car, his eyes seeming to narrow on the man who was even now stepping out of it. His expression eased into a half smile. "Yah."

"Well, I guess you'd best go and find out." It took all she had to keep her voice from choking. "I'll let you and Becky out at the lane. Star will be fine going home."

"He will, for sure." Aaron spoke absently, all his attention on the man who waited for him.

He pulled up at the lane, getting down quickly and helping Becky down. Without even a goodbye, he strode off toward the house.

Sally turned the buggy into her lane, clucking to Star. Thank the good Lord she hadn't lost control where he could see her. Now she could let the tears flow. His employer would want him back, and in a moment he'd be gone. It was over.

Chapter Fifteen

Aaron walked toward Albert Winfield, his mind racing. Was this a good sign? The man didn't look angry, but did his presence mean he was ready to believe in Aaron? At least he wasn't wearing the furious, judgmental expression that had been stamped on his face during their final interview in his office. That was encouraging.

Becky, seeming excited about the presence of an Englisch visitor, ran ahead. Then she came to a stop, spun and raced back to Aaron. Her brief spurt of courage had vanished as her shyness took over.

Aaron took her hand, as much for his own comfort as hers. Was she picking up on his apprehension? He hoped not. Hand in hand, they walked up to Mr. Winfield. Becky studied her shoes, and Aaron met the man's eyes firmly, not willing to be the first to extend his hand.

"Aaron. I'm glad to see you." Winfield tore his gaze from Aaron and bent to smile at Becky clinging to Aaron's hand. "Who's this? Will you introduce me?"

"This is my niece, Becky. Becky, this is Mr. Winfield. I used to work for him."

Winfield had been staring because he'd never seen Aaron in Amish clothing before, he supposed. The black pants, solid blue shirt, suspenders and straw hat were pretty much a uniform here, but would seem strange to Winfield.

Becky emerged from her study of her feet to give Winfield a fleeting smile.

Aaron patted her head. "Run on in to your mammi," he said, using Pennsylvania Dutch.

Nodding, Becky scurried toward the back door, but before she could reach it, it opened. "Aaron, was ist…" Jessie let the words trail off, looking at the stranger.

Aaron filled her in quickly in Pennsylvania Dutch, and then switched to English. "Mr. Winfield, this is Jessie King, my brother Caleb's wife."

Winfield removed his ball cap, polite as always. "Nice to know you, Mrs. King."

"You are wilkom, Mr. Winfield." Her eyes were wary, and relief swept over her face when Caleb and Onkel Zeb came around the corner of the house, probably because they'd seen the strange car.

Aaron performed the introductions again, suppressing the urge to laugh. If Winfield was dismayed by the appearance of so many Amish, to say nothing of their cautious response to him, he hid it.

What was Caleb thinking? Did he suspect that his brother was about to leave them again? But Caleb's steady gaze held only support.

An awkward silence fell, and he didn't know how to break it. Finally Onkel Zeb spoke.

"You will want to talk to Aaron, ain't so? If you'll come inside, you can be comfortable. We'll leave you two alone."

"Well, thanks, but I don't want to put you folks out. I could stand to stretch my legs after that long drive. Aaron, how about taking a walk around with me?"

A sensible solution that he should have thought of himself. It would get them away from an audience. "Sure. Let's go up toward the orchard." He gestured toward the fruit trees on the slope beyond the barn.

Winfield gave the family a polite nod, and Aaron led the way across the yard and through the field. They walked in silence for a few minutes, the grassy pathway muffling their footsteps.

When they reached the orchard, Mr. Winfield paused, smiling a little as he studied the still-laden apple trees. Aaron reached up and plucked a ripe cooking apple, inhaling the sweet scent of it.

A flash of memory went through him, triggered by the smell…a small version of himself climbing into the tree to toss down apples to his mother, standing below. She caught them in her apron, looking up at him with a carefree laugh.

The image unnerved him. He'd managed to bury the memories of a time when his mother had still been a part of his life. All three of them had, he supposed, once she'd left them.

Winfield was gazing over the farm, spread out below them. "It's a mighty pretty place. Reminds me of where I grew up. Your brother's, is it?"

He nodded. Funny, but he hadn't thought of how the property had been left. Caleb was the one who had kept it going no matter what had happened in their lives, so in that sense it was his, but in another way, it belonged to all of them—to everyone who had sprung from it and loved it.

"I guess I'd better get to the point." Winfield shoved his hands in his pockets and hunched his shoulders. "I was mighty glad to get that letter from you. I'd been looking for you, but nobody seemed to know where you'd gone."

Aaron's eyebrows lifted. "You'd been looking for me?"

"Yeah. It was this way, you see." He cleared his throat, seeming to have difficulty getting started. "Well, once I cooled down, I knew I'd been rash, accusing you before I'd looked into things on my own."

Aaron wouldn't nod agreement, but he felt his expression tighten.

Winfield probably noticed. "So I started with what I knew. The horse had been doped, no question of that. But you weren't the only one who could have gotten at him."

"No, I wasn't." He kept his voice neutral, but that, after all, was what had stung the most…that the man he'd respected had rushed to judge him without investigating.

"Sorry." Winfield sent a shamefaced look his way and went back to studying the landscape. "Well, I started asking around, and Joe

Miller came to see me. He wasn't happy, Joe wasn't. Why would you do that? That's what he said, and it got me to thinking."

He hadn't even considered the question of who the guilty party was. Someone had done it, and it had to be someone with access to Winfield Stables shortly before the race.

"Only one of us who worked there could get in on race day," Aaron said.

Winfield nodded. "And nobody there had reason to want us to lose, unless they were paid off. So I started looking for someone who had more cash than he should have. Joe helped me." He grimaced. "It wasn't hard, not with Pete Foster buying drinks for everyone down at the Rusty Anchor all night, when he usually didn't have two cents to rub together."

It fit, now that Aaron thought of it. Foster was one of the few stablemen who didn't really seem to care all that much for the animals he tended. It was just a job for him, that's all.

"Did he admit it?"

"Yeah, he did. He folded as soon as the racing commission started asking questions. Ended up with sanctions against Norton Stables and a hefty fine for them. Just wish I thought it would make them act straight from now on." He shrugged, turning toward Aaron.

"So, I'm here to say I'm sorry. That comes first. I acted wrongly toward you, Aaron, and I hope you can forgive me."

Aaron paused, searching for the anger and resentment he'd had when he got back to Lost Creek. It wasn't there. Smiling, he held out his hand. "It's forgotten. We're okay."

Winfield shook his hand vigorously, beaming. "I'm glad, mighty glad you see it that way. Now for the rest of it—I want you to come back. Not just as head trainer, but also manager. With a raise, of course."

Manager of an outfit as big as Winfield Stables— that meant something. It was what he'd wanted, but still, he hesitated.

"I don't expect your answer now," Winfield added. "You'll need time. Take all the time you need."

"Denke—thank you, I mean. My family… Well, I should talk to them."

He didn't quite know why he'd said that, but he realized it was true. He hadn't talked to anyone when he'd run away, and he'd left a lot of hurt behind. He couldn't do it that way again.

And there was Sally.

They started slowly back down, the grass brushing against Aaron's pant legs and the scents of autumn rising from the land. Familiar. Everything about this place was familiar, right down to the blades of grass. The day he came back he'd resented that familiarity. Now...

Now it swept over him in a flood, stopping him in his tracks. He'd left here once, called away by the lure of the unknown. He'd looked for a place for himself out there in the world.

But now he felt a call that went bone-deep, beyond any possibility of question. The land itself called to him. He knew, with a certainty that was beyond words, that what he wanted was here...here in the verdant hills, the fruitful trees and the golden wash of autumn sunlight across the fields.

Here, where he had roots, and where work waited for him that only he could do. Where people loved him and belonged to him.

And Sally. The place where he belonged had been here all along, waiting for him to open his eyes, his ears and his heart to find it. There were no more questions. He was at peace.

The sun was slipping toward the top of the ridge as Sally walked to the barn. Its slanting rays turned the leaves to brilliant shades of yellow and red where they struck. Even with her heart breaking, she could be thankful for the beauty of the valley where God had placed them.

But in a few minutes, the sun would slide behind the hill and darkness would creep over the valley. The air would grow chilly, and she'd be as cold outside as she was inside.

Sally stepped into the barn, stopping for a moment to let her eyes grow accustomed to the dim light. Star poked his head over the stall and gave a whicker of welcome.

She went to him, patting him and holding out the carrot he expected. "Greedy boy," she murmured. Her throat tightened. "Ach, I should talk. I'm greedy, too, crying over what I can't have instead of thanking God for what I do."

Star moved his head up and down, brushing against her. She'd fancy he agreed with her, but she knew he only wanted his face rubbed. Trying to smile, she complied, and his eyes closed in bliss.

"You're easily made happy, ain't so?"

She leaned her forehead against the stall post, holding back the tears that kept threatening to overwhelm her. Strange, that even

Elizabeth had seemed to know this wasn't a time to try and make her feel better.

Instead, she'd given Sally an extra-large serving of potpie and shushed Ben when he started to wonder when Aaron might leave. No question but that she and Elizabeth had reached a new understanding. She just regretted that it had come at the cost of so much pain.

Sally wished she could believe that Aaron's leaving wasn't already decided. But when she'd seen the way he'd headed toward the Englischer without a backward glance, she'd known. He'd go back to that other life.

So she would stay here, filling up the hole in her heart with family, faith and the scholars who meant so much to her. It was a good life. A satisfying, useful life. But not the one she'd hoped for.

"Ach, Star, why am I so foolish?"

"What are you feeling foolish about?"

For an instant Sally stared at Star as if the gelding had spoken to her. Then she turned toward the doorway. Aaron stood there, a dark silhouette against the golden light behind him. The moment seemed to freeze into an image that burned into her mind.

Aaron moved toward her, the image becoming reality. He crossed the space between them in a few steps and then stopped an arm's length away.

"I... I thought you'd gone." It was all she could manage. She had visualized him on the road back to that other life so clearly that she could barely grasp his presence.

He shook his head. "Winfield is gone. He left after supper."

"But I thought..." she stammered to a halt. Maybe Aaron had needed time—time to make things right with his family, time to prepare for leaving.

"I would never go away without saying goodbye." He paused, his gaze on her face. "And I can't possibly say goodbye."

The truth began to dawn on her, so longed for that she didn't dare believe it. "You can't?"

"I can't, because I'm not going. This is home." There was a certainty in his deep voice that she hadn't heard before. "This is where I belong. I know that now."

Wait...take it slowly. She had to be sure. *He* had to be sure. "Are you certain sure of that?"

He smiled, ever so slightly...just a hint of that teasing smile she cherished. "Doubts, Sally? Yah, I'm certain sure." He reached across the space between them to take her hand, holding it as if it tethered him to this spot. "I didn't know myself until I had the chance to go back. And then I knew."

Quick understanding flooded her. "Your boss...your friend...he believes you now. That's what you wanted."

"He believes me, yah. It's like you said— quick to anger, and just as quick to regret. Once he cooled off, he took the time to find the truth. He asked me to come back with a raise and promotion. But I turned it down."

She could scarcely take a breath. Now it was his grasp that tethered her.

"It was just like the bishop said. If I waited and listened with an open heart, the Lord would show me what was right." Aaron's voice thickened with emotion. "I stood there looking at the farm with his offer in my ears, and all I could hear was the call to stay—as if each separate blade of grass and clump of soil was calling out that here is where I belong."

Her heart was almost too full for speech. "I... I am happy for you."

The tug of his hand brought them closer. "Don't you see? Everything I want is here... including you, if you'll have me. Will you, Sally?"

She could only look into his eyes, word-less. Her answer must have been written in her face, because he closed the gap between them in a heartbeat, and his lips found hers.

The world closed into the warm, protective, cherishing circle of Aaron's arms. The kiss spoke of shared love and tenderness. Of commitment. Of belonging to each other as long as life should last.

When their lips parted at last, she felt that everything important had been said between them. And she was sure enough to be willing to tease him, just a little.

"You know what this means, don't you? You can't get out of it. You're going to be kneeling in front of the entire church."

He dropped a kiss on the tip of her nose. "You'll enjoy that, won't you?"

He might mean it lightly, but she realized in that instant that it was even more true than he thought. "*Enjoy* might not be the right word." She tilted her face up to his. "*Rejoicing* would be better. We will all rejoice."

"Yah, I guess you will." He almost sounded surprised. "The bishop was right about that, too. He said that part came at the end, not the beginning. I see it now. He knew that once God had His way with me, asking forgiveness and accepting it would be something to look forward to, not to reject."

She nodded, heart full. "You're not dreading it any longer?"

"No, never. It was only pride that held me back, always pride." He seemed to struggle for words. "I understand now. There's no room for pride in love. I'm sorry it took me so long."

There was no room for pride in love. It was exactly what she'd learned, too. God had dealt with both of them.

"It was worth it." She put her palm against his cheek, feeling the connection that flowed back and forth between them, sure and strong. "We still have a lot to look forward to…a whole lifetime of being together."

He turned his head slightly to press a kiss against her palm. "And a lot for me to make up. I need to court you properly, don't I?"

"That's right. Every single step." Her joy was spilling over, making her want to laugh for sheer pleasure.

His arms tightened around her again. "Then we should start with another kiss, ain't so?"

Holding him close, she gave herself to the kiss…a kiss that held all the promise of a life together, blessed by God, who had brought them so surely to this moment. They were both home where they belonged.

Epilogue

"You will be next, ain't so?" Onkel Zeb put a hand on Aaron's shoulder as they stood together for a moment, out of the crowd of people who packed the Fisher farmhouse to celebrate the marriage of Daniel and Rebecca.

"I will."

Aaron figured about a dozen people had said that to him in the past hour, and there would be many more before the day was over. Instead of annoying him, it gave him a fresh spurt of joy each time. In a few months, he and Sally would belong to each other in the sight of God and the church.

"A spring wedding will be gut, even if it's not traditional." Onkel Zeb set his seal of approval on their plans. "Sally will want to finish out the school year." He sent a cautious glance toward Aaron. "She will miss her scholars, ain't so?"

"Yah, she will." The subject didn't hold any secrets…he and Sally had discussed it thoroughly. "She hopes…we both hope that we'll start a family soon, and she'll have our own kinder to teach and care for. And later, once they're bigger, she'll be able to go back to teaching again."

The custom was that teachers were young, unmarried women, but that was just the way it had been in their district, not the way it must be. And Sally was born to teach.

A small figure hurtled out of the door behind them, almost tripping. Aaron caught Lige before he could go headlong, and set him on his feet.

"Denke, Onkel Aaron." He said the words with a shy smile. "You're my onkel now, too, ain't so?"

"I am, for sure. We are all family now."

"Yah." The boy beamed. "I'm glad." He hurried off again, bound on some errand of his own, most likely.

"Families coming together and new families starting. That's how life is meant to be." Onkel Zeb had a satisfied look on his face. "And we will set to rest forever the idea that the King men are unfortunate in love, ain't so?"

"For sure." Aaron said the simple words with feeling. To see Daniel and Rebecca claim each other in marriage today had moved his heart. He longed for the moment when he and Sally would be the ones taking that step in the presence of the church.

His gaze, moving across the tables of guests, came to rest on Sally, who was giving some directions to those serving. As if she felt the touch of his look, she turned her head to smile at him. Their eyes met, communicating without a spoken word from across the room.

Onkel Zeb elbowed him. "What are you doing wasting time with me? Go and help your sweetheart."

"Gut idea," he said, and slipped through the forest of chairs and tables, narrowly missing a collision with a teenager carrying a laden tray.

Coming to his rescue, Sally caught his hand and led him out a door. He found they were in a short hall between the kitchen and the pantry. Alone in the hall. Taking advantage of the moment, he stole a quick kiss.

Sally looked up at him, her face saucy. "I thought you wanted to see me."

"I did," he protested. "I needed a kiss. And

maybe, since we're alone for a moment, a second one." He suited the action to the words.

After a satisfying moment, Sally reached up to drop a kiss on his chin. "Won't be long until you're growing a beard. Sure you won't miss the clean-shaven look?"

He rubbed his chin. "I think I'll look wonderful gut with a beard, don't you?"

"Fishing for a compliment? Yah, I'm so besotted with you that I'd think you looked handsome no matter what."

"That's as it should be. After all, I look considerably different now than when you were first promised to me."

For once he had the satisfaction of seeing Sally at a loss. "Different?" Her face was puzzled.

"You forgot," he said, shaking his head. "I'm surprised at you. You must have been at least eleven or twelve when I said I'd wait for you to grow up and marry you. Don't you remember?"

"Teasing again," she said in her best teacher voice. "The teacher might have to make you stand in the corner."

"That's all right." He snuggled his arms around her. "As long as you're there with me."

She responded with the gurgle of laughter

he loved, and Aaron's heart swelled. Little had he known, that day he'd walked down the road with his heart filled with bitterness, just how much joy waited for him here.

This was what their life together would be like—filled with joy and laughter and no doubt their share of sorrow. But whatever the future brought, God would bring them through it together, so long as they were faithful.

* * * * *

If you enjoyed this story,
don't miss the previous books in the
Brides of Lost Creek series
from Marta Perry:

Second Chance Amish Bride
The Wedding Quilt Bride

And be sure to pick up
Amish Christmas Blessings
from Love Inspired, featuring Marta Perry's
The Midwife's Christmas Surprise

Find more great reads at
www.LoveInspired.com.

Dear Reader,

Welcome to the third book in the Brides of Lost Creek series, *The Promised Amish Bride*. Sally Stoltzfus was just a child when the neighbor she adored, Aaron King, ran away to the Englisch world. Sally was left with the memory of a lighthearted promise...that when she grew up, Aaron would marry her. When Aaron comes back, life takes unexpected turns for many people in Lost Creek.

I love stories of first loves finding fulfillment, so this story was a joy to write. I hope you enjoy reading it as much as I enjoyed writing it. And that you'll come back again for future stories set in Lost Creek.

Let me know if you enjoy my story. You can find me online at www.martaperry.com, on Facebook at www.Facebook.com/martaperrybooks, or you can email me at mpjohn@ptd.net. I'll be happy to respond with a signed bookmark and my brochure of Pennsylvania Dutch recipes.

Blessings,
Marta Perry

Get 4 FREE REWARDS!

We'll send you 2 FREE Books plus 2 FREE Mystery Gifts.

Love Inspired® Suspense books feature Christian characters facing challenges to their faith... and lives.

FREE Value Over $20

Get 4 FREE REWARDS!

We'll send you 2 FREE Books plus 2 FREE Mystery Gifts.

Harlequin® Heartwarming™ Larger-Print books feature traditional values of home, family, community and—most of all—love.

FREE Value Over $20

YES! Please send me 2 FREE Harlequin® Heartwarming™ Larger-Print novels and my 2 FREE mystery gifts (gifts worth about $10 retail). After receiving them, if I don't wish to receive any more books, I can return the shipping statement marked "cancel." If I don't cancel, I will receive 4 brand-new larger-print novels every month and be billed just $5.49 per book in the U.S. or $6.24 per book in Canada. That's a savings of at least 19% off the cover price. It's quite a bargain! Shipping and handling is just 50¢ per book in the U.S. and 75¢ per book in Canada.* I understand that accepting the 2 free books and gifts places me under no obligation to buy anything. I can always return a shipment and cancel at any time. The free books and gifts are mine to keep no matter what I decide.

161/361 IDN GMY3

Name (please print)

Address   Apt. #

City   State/Province   Zip/Postal Code

> **Mail to the Reader Service:**
> **IN U.S.A.:** P.O. Box 1341, Buffalo, NY 14240-8531
> **IN CANADA:** P.O. Box 603, Fort Erie, Ontario L2A 5X3

Want to try 2 free books from another series! Call 1-800-873-8635 or visit www.ReaderService.com.

*Terms and prices subject to change without notice. Prices do not include sales taxes, which will be charged (if applicable) based on your state or country of residence. Canadian residents will be charged applicable taxes. Offer not valid in Quebec. This offer is limited to one order per household. Books received may not be as shown. Not valid for current subscribers to Harlequin Heartwarming Larger-Print books. All orders subject to approval. Credit or debit balances in a customer's account(s) may be offset by any other outstanding balance owed by or to the customer. Please allow 4 to 6 weeks for delivery. Offer available while quantities last.

Your Privacy—The Reader Service is committed to protecting your privacy. Our Privacy Policy is available online at www.ReaderService.com or upon request from the Reader Service. We make a portion of our mailing list available to reputable third parties that offer products we believe may interest you. If you prefer that we not exchange your name with third parties, or if you wish to clarify or modify your communication preferences, please visit us at www.ReaderService.com/consumerschoice or write to us at Reader Service Preference Service, P.O. Box 9062, Buffalo, NY 14240-9062. Include your complete name and address.

HW19R

MUST ♥ DOGS COLLECTION

SAVE 30% AND GET A FREE GIFT!

Finding true love can be "ruff"— but not when adorable dogs help to play matchmaker in these inspiring romantic "tails."

YES! Please send me the first shipment of four books from the **Must ♥ Dogs Collection**. If I don't cancel, I will continue to receive four books a month for two additional months, and I will be billed at the same discount price of $18.20 U.S./$20.30 CAN., plus $1.99 for shipping and handling.* That's a 30% discount off the cover prices! Plus, I'll receive a FREE adorable, hand-painted dog figurine in every shipment (approx. retail value of $4.99)! I am under no obligation to purchase anything and I may cancel at any time by marking "cancel" on the shipping statement and returning the shipment. I may keep the FREE books no matter what I decide.

☐ 256 HCN 4331   ☐ 456 HCN 4331

Name (please print)

Address   Apt. #

City   State/Province   Zip/Postal Code

Mail to the Reader Service:
IN U.S.A.: P.O. Box 1867, Buffalo, NY. 14240-1867
IN CANADA: P.O. Box 609, Fort Erie, Ontario L2A 5X3

PETSBPA19

READERSERVICE.COM

Manage your account online!

- Review your order history
- Manage your payments
- Update your address

> ### We've designed the Reader Service website just for you.

Enjoy all the features!

- Discover new series available to you, and read excerpts from any series.
- Respond to mailings and special monthly offers.
- Browse the Bonus Bucks catalog and online-only exculsives.
- Share your feedback.

Visit us at:

ReaderService.com